The Heart of Dixie

TATE PUBLISHING
AND ENTERPRISES, LLC

Published by Tate Publishing & Enterprises, LLC
127 E. Trade Center Terrace | Mustang, Oklahoma 73064 USA
1.888.361.9473 | www.tatepublishing.com

Tate Publishing is committed to excellence in the publishing industry. The company reflects the philosophy established by the founders, based on Psalm 68:11,
"The Lord gave the word and great was the company of those who published it."

Book design copyright © 2013 by Tate Publishing, LLC. All rights reserved.
Cover design by Rtor Maghuyop
Interior design by Jake Muelle

Published in the United States of America

ISBN: 978-1-62854-217-2
1. Fiction / Christian / Romance
2. Fiction / Christian / General
13.10.30

Acknowledgments

This book would never have been attempted if I didn't have a love of reading. I started reading at a very young age and was sneaking my mom's romance novels as early as first grade. My primary goal in reading was to gain knowledge and, of course, be entertained. Lucky for me, God blessed me with parents that chose to nurture this desire in me. They bought the complete set of Childcraft and Britannica Encyclopedias, and I methodically worked my way through them. For this, my first thank you goes to my Mom and Dad. They are amazing people.

The following people read my manuscript through the various stages and gave me invaluable advice: Tracy Curtis, my amazing and gorgeous sister-in-law, Alan Simmons, who is a published author and inspired me in so many ways, Darlene Harris, who is my best friend and the wisest person I know, and Tammy McCause, who is a fabulous friend and tells me the truth. Thank you all for being there for me.

My favorite person in the world is my daughter, Erika. She is a warrior in every sense of the word and I draw inspiration from her in aspects of every character I create. She is God's greatest gift to me.

My husband is a man after God's own heart. He would do anything for me and our combined three daughters–Erika, Jenifer, and Bethany. He is a true man who can be found building furniture, fishing, and singing "Soft Kitty" to our granddaughter in the same day. Oh, and he happens to have gorgeous blue eyes...

Prologue

I am so lost in my own thoughts that I barely register that the pastor has stopped speaking. I look up through my veil and see that he is gesturing me to come stand next to the closed casket that represents the body of my dead husband. It suddenly seems ridiculous that we are all pretending that he wasn't blown into a thousand pieces and sunk to the bottom of the Mississippi River and that the stupid coffin is just symbolic. I feel an irrational urge to laugh but manage to cover it with a small cough as I make my way up to stand next to the pastor and my in-laws.

I am extremely grateful for the black lace veil I'm wearing; this way, I don't have to acknowledge the gestures of sympathy coming from people I don't know and don't necessarily like. My husband's family never liked me and liked me even less when I gave away so much of what they considered their son's money. Never mind that it came from my hard work. The other people here are mostly David's coworkers, who are only sorry for the fact that David's death came from an event that will end up costing the company billions of dollars.

After shaking an enormous amount of hands, the funeral is over. I now only have to make it through the burial before I can leave and not have to see these people again. The only reason I'm here at all is out of respect for the baby girl I will be bringing into the world in just a couple of months. She's losing her father before she's born—another victim of this tragedy.

When the last people have come through and made their way out of the soaring doors of this huge old church, my bodyguard comes to take my arm and lead me out.

I'm still furious that I have something as ridiculous as a bodyguard. The waste treatment plant explosion that killed my husband also caused an epic waterway contamination, which has the environmentalist groups up in arms. An actor that I've never heard of before has made the destruction of David's reputation his personal mission and had just recently taken to making up horrid stories about me. The ensuing publicity and numerous death threats had driven David's employer to insist upon providing me with security.

Outside, I take a lungful of humid Memphis air, and I'm glad that even with the sunny skies, the temperature isn't too oppressive. Between the pregnancy and the black mourning outfit, I'm struggling as it is. Halfway down the sidewalk to the waiting hearse, I have a sudden thought.

"Sam, will you take a look inside the car and make sure no one else is in there? I want it to be just you and I. Understand?" Sam has been with me just a few days, and he already gets the rocky relationship the Beauregard's and I have. He nods and walks over to the waiting vehicle and leans in.

Just then I see movement to my right and turn to see a pretty young woman walking up to me. Her blonde hair shines in the sun, and she has freckles across her cheeks. She is wearing a patchwork skirt with a T-shirt bearing the image of a man I feel like I should recognize. In her hands, she has a beautiful white teddy bear that has a large yellow bow on it.

She holds it out in front of her, and instinctively, I reach up to take it from her. She smiles sweetly and simply says, "For the baby."

I barely have time to say thank you before she sprints off back the way she came. There is a small tag hanging from the neck, and I tuck the bear up under one arm to read it. It says, "Rexanna Beauregard, tell your husband hello."

I start to frown and then my world disappears with a loud bang and haze of horrific pain and the smell of burning flesh. The last conscious thought I have is when the name of the man's face on the girl's T-shirt comes to mind—Mason McCoy.

One

" **S**o what'd'ya'll think?" the rouged, bouffant-haired, former beauty queen real-estate agent asks. She makes the word *think* sound like *thank*. She is beautiful and kind and makes me feel like the most special person in the world. In other words, she is perfect at her job.

In this case, Miss Cotton Fest 2005 is totally wasting her talents. The beach cottage is perfect. As if someone had plucked it from my imagination, here it sits with a giant live oak in the front yard, shading a quaint front porch. The inside is an open concept with the only closed off areas on the bottom floor being two bedrooms across the back and a full bathroom. The centered floating stairs lead to an upper level loft and another full bathroom. The very best part is the huge screened-in sleeping porch off the back of the house. It was in massive state of disrepair, but I was thrilled with the potential.

"I think I'll take it, Ms. Gibson," I say with a smile.

"Reeeaaallly?" she squeals. Then letting her façade down for a minute, she lets out a hoot and grabs me in a hug. It's at that very moment that I decided I have made my first friend in Bay St. Louis, Mississippi.

"Yes, really, and no messing around. I want to make a full price offer. My only request is that they leave the furniture pieces that are on the sleeping porch and that I want to close the transaction by the first of next week."

Twenty minutes later, I'm back on I-10 headed toward New Orleans. I'm staying there until the deal is done, and I can move into the cottage. I have a pied-a-terre above an antique shop in the French Quarter that I have owned for several years. I used to own homes in Memphis and Boston with my husband, but those were sold years before.

As I feel the familiar melancholy start fogging my brain, I reach down and turn my iPod on to an upbeat playlist and smile as the comfortable sounds of the Red Rocker, Sammy Hagar, come pouring through the speakers of my Audi S5 Cabriolet. Once again, I wonder if I'm doing the right thing by moving to the Mississippi Coast in order to be close to *him*. Unbidden, his face pops up in my mind's eye and my stomach clenches and my blood begins to boil. Subconsciously, my foot presses harder on the accelerator, and the 333 horses oblige happily. Before I know it, I've hit one hundred miles per hour, and I feel a giddy rise in my adrenaline. Slowly I bring both the car and my temper back under control. This is something I have gone over and over with myself, and I know that I have to forgive this man. I have to if I am going to be able to move forward in my life. The bitterness that I hold toward him is, in the words of a wise pastor I heard speak once, like me drinking poison and waiting for him to die. I am being eaten from the inside out, and that peasant is living his wonderful, glamorous life and doesn't even know or care that I am suffering. Well, I have to change that, and the only way I know how to is to get to know him through his home, the people who love him, and who knows maybe even him. Perhaps I can somehow, someway, find something redeemable in him to like and make myself forgive him.

The good news is that he doesn't know who I am. He knows full well what he did, just not that it was me on the receiving end. The bad news is that he is in the public eye and therefore not the most accessible person on earth.

I feel sure it will happen though. I've been praying about it for months. After all, this is why I'm here at this point. My belief in God has been part of my life since I can remember, but belief and relationship are two very different things.

After the events of the past few years I turned to Him, first to scream and yell at Him then because I thought I was about to meet Him and then because He was the only one I trusted. The relationship grew, but for it to really develop, I had to get over my hurt and bitterness. I became fully aware that without forgiveness, I was not going to be able to have any closure or growth, and I need both of those things in a way that only shows itself in the deepest, darkest hours of the night when I find myself on my knees with my face on the cold stones of my floor with tears and self-loathing flowing freely as I beg for understanding and forgiveness of my own.

I come out of my dark thoughts as I pull up to the courtyard entrance and enter the code for entry into the private parking area. Rather than go up to the flat, I walk down to the Funky Pelican. Giles sees me as I walk in and waves me up to the stage. I slide in and pull the lonely cello between my legs and pick up on an updated version of "Mr. Five by Five." I completely lose myself in the music as we play one after the other. This has become my routine on five out of seven nights every week I have been in town these past seven months. The owner of the bar is a woman named Cindy. I met her through a couple, Paul and Randy, who were sicced on me by the man who gave me refuge in Costa Rica after *it* happened. Over drinks one night, it came out that I could play several instruments, and Cindy asked if I would want to fill in on occasion. On occasion turned into most weeknights, and I am thrilled with that. I won't take money, and I play whichever instrument is open—piano, cello, bass, or acoustic guitar. I occasionally even play fiddle when the piece calls for it. One of my five degrees is in musical performance and direction, but the ability to play musical instruments and sing has been part of my life as long as I can remember.

I've never made a living off this ability, but that is all about to change. I smile as I think of this because I never dreamed of doing something I actually *loved* as a career. It dawns on me—as I stand up and take the mic to sing "Don't You Know"—that ironically, I have Mr. Mason McCoy to thank for that.

Two

Two days later, I get a call from Michelle Gibson from Gulf Properties to let me know that my offer has been accepted and that we can close the following Monday.

"That is fantastic news, Michelle. Thank you so much for making this happen for me."

"Are you kidding, honey? How often do you think someone walks in and buys a fixer-upper with no negotiation and then pays cash?" She and I both chuckle at that.

"One day, Dixie, I would love to spend some time hearing all about what brought you here. I just know you have a fascinating story."

"Well, I don't know about fascinating, but I'll try not to disappoint you." I give what I hope is a convincing snort, but then I do something I've wanted to do since I met Michelle. "Seriously, can we get together for lunch or dinner Monday? Maybe we can just be a couple of girls, you know, discuss who's hotter, Adam Levine or Gerard Butler, and you can fill me in on the town secrets."

"I thought you'd never ask!" she says and then gets serious. "You need to know, though, that I'm more of

15

a Channing Tatum girl myself." She giggles in that awesome girlish way she has.

After hanging up, I make another call to the principal of the BSL High School to let her know my plans and then call the banks to make the necessary transfers of funds. For the next few days, I make plans for a small moving van and start looking at local companies in the gulf area that specialize in reclaimed and ecological material for building materials. I am going to need some new furniture.

For the first time in a long time, I have something to look forward to. It's a great feeling.

Three

My feet make slapping sounds on the boardwalk as I run full speed along the beach. The sounds of the Thomas Tallis scholars singing "Spem in Alium" fill my head, and I turn toward the historical depot section of downtown Bay St. Louis. I've been in my cottage for two weeks, working on it like a fiend, and I'm in love with this town and the people here. I feel so relaxed and am looking forward to the next chapter of my life. I still haven't formulated a plan to get to run into Mason McCoy or even been able to find out how often he comes home, but I trust that the Father will guide me. I say a quick prayer, my daily prayer, that when I do see McCoy, I'll be able to see him as Christ sees him. I know it's the only way.

As I come to a string of store fronts, a beautiful window display catches my eye. It contains some gorgeous handcrafted furniture pieces, each containing a hand carved fleur-de-lis. I stop, jogging in place as I stare mesmerized at the pieces. The name of the business is Just Old Barnwood, and the tagline suggests everything is made from reclaimed or recycled wood. I am instantly charmed, and think I have found the right place to create my new bed and doors for my hallway washer/dryer.

As I'm standing there, stretching and bending and committing the name and number of the store to memory, I see movement in the background of the huge picture window. I freeze as I realize belatedly that I'm being watched. It is just after 7 a.m. on a Thursday morning, the business doesn't open until nine, so no one should be there! I prepare to take off quickly, moving my hand to the small canister in my arm band to make sure I can reach it if need be.

The person in the store moves forward and the panic recedes as I realize it's someone that works there, coming to the window, having seen that I am staring and drooling like a madwoman. I flush, embarrassed, feeling like a voyeur. As the door unlocks and chimes and is held open, a cool, low voice speaks from the relative dark and says, "Come on in, and have a look around if you'd like."

As the light comes on I first freeze and then clench my eyes shut behind my sunglasses as I realize it's *him*. His black hair is sticking up all over his head. He has not shaved in several days, but both his arrogant blue eyes and irreverent tone are impossible to miss.

No, no, no! I'm not ready for this and besides, what in the heck is he doing here in this amazing store with these amazing works of art?

Four

The interior comes alive as he turns on the overhead lights. I gasp as the true beauty of the pieces comes to life. I love the rawness that I see here, and I know that I have to have this for my little home. Something speaks in my heart, my soul, and my brain.

"So see something you need?" the smooth, dulcet toned voice asks, and I feel the low notes deep in my body. His mouth is set in a smirk, and I know he is keenly aware of his sexual affect on women and most likely relishes it. I am sweaty all over from my early morning run and fully aware that my hair has escaped in a hundred spots from my braid. However, his eyes are glued to my lips, and I know that he can't see my eyes behind my large Oakley sunglasses. I go to slide them up on my head, and out of nowhere a dozen trumpets blare in my head and my vision goes dark. Just before I hit the ground, a pair of strong arms catch me and lowers me to the floor.

I don't know how long I was out, but when I come to, I am staring into blue eyes filled with genuine concern. They are so kind and expressive that I simply stare for several beats until they crinkle up at the sides and the mouth a few inches below them quirks up in a smile then speaks.

"Are you okay? You scared the crap outta me!"

It takes a second for it all to come back to me because I am stunned anew at the sweetness in this man's face. In my brain, I know who he is, but I can't for the life of me bring the gritty emotions I was feeling before to the surface. I feel as if my bones have turned to taffy, and I am no longer in control of my person. Let's see if I can speak.

"Mmmhmmm." Oh, surely I can do better than that. I clear my throat and try again. "Yes, I mean, yes, I'm okay. At least, I think I'm okay. I can't seem to move."

"What?" Now he's freaking out, and that brings me out of my weird stupor. I turn my head and look at my hand, which I bring up to feel my head.

"Never mind," I say as I move into a sitting position. "I've had this happen before. It's from an old injury to my ear. I have occasional fainting spells."

He pulls a chair over and helps me up into it and tells me to stay put while he literally runs through a door behind us. In seconds, he is back with a coffee mug filled with water. I raise my eyebrow.

"I know, I know, but it's the best I have. We're a green business, so it's not like we keep bottled water around."

"I guess that would be a little hypocritical, huh?"

"Yep," he says, and he blows his breath up into his bangs and slides his hands into his back pockets. "And I've had enough of that to fill a lifetime."

We look at each other for a few beats and then I stand and put the mug down. "I think I'm okay now."

I say and smile at him because I can't help myself. Something similar to a tectonic plate shift has happened deep down in my soul, and I am anxious to get home and meditate on what God might be doing here.

He looks unconvinced, but rather than saying so, he just takes a couple steps closer, positioned to catch me should I fall again.

"I'm glad to hear it. I'm sorry for whatever happened to cause your injury. I can see the scars since you mentioned it but barely."

When he says this, the irony of the moment almost buckles my knees again. The sheer compassion he is showing me, a stranger who stumbled into his shop, too bad he hadn't had some of that for Rexanna Beauregard. I can't help it. My eyes fill with tears, and I have to find a distraction. I look away at some of the art hanging on the wall.

"I love this shop. There are several framed pieces I believe I'll have to come back for," I say as I look back over my shoulder at the art in question. As I turn my head back around, I see that his eyes are tracking the trail of my tear. It makes me flush, and I swipe angrily at my cheek to remove the offending liquid. "But more importantly, I'm in need of a custom-built bed frame, a desk, and two sliding barn-style doors for my hall laundry. I really like the look of recycled materials, and I completely love what I see here."

"Do you have the dimensions for the bed and the doors, miss…?"

"Bryan. Dixie Bryan."

"Miss Bryan."

"Yes. Uh, no, actually I don't. I've just moved into a cottage I bought over on Beach Boulevard, and I don't have any measurements. Do you think your carpenter could come by and take them for me?" I ask. I swallow hard because it is beginning to dawn on me that this entire encounter is exactly what I wanted and what I prayed for. Who would have ever thought I would meet Mason McCoy on my first foray into town? We do indeed serve a Mighty God.

"I'm sure we could arrange that. Do you mind leaving your address and phone number here, and one of us will contact you for a time to come by and get that information from you?" he asks.

As I write my address and phone number down on a contact sheet, I feel his eyes boring into the top of my head. I can tell he is intrigued by me, and I am intrigued as all get out as to why he is in this amazing store and why I've reacted this way.

As soon as I write down my address, he jerks his head up and looks more intently at me.

"Something wrong?" I ask.

He hesitates for a second and then says, "No, no. It's just that it appears you don't live very far from where I stay when I'm in town."

"Oh." I don't really know what else to say, so I murmur my good-byes, and I hastily put my copy of the work order into my fanny pack and make my departure. I test my return to health by running the remaining mile of my route to the cottage and sit on the front porch with a cup of Community Coffee. The sun has tinged the gulf a beautiful pinkish orange, and the breeze dries the sweat on my arms and legs and gives me a case of the goose bumps. I feel off-kilter from my run-in with Mason McCoy. It was so unexpected, and I wasn't prepared. My defenses weren't up. How could my body and emotions react that way to a man that I have hated for so long? Pure treachery!

On the plus side, if he has something to do with that magnificent store, it could be a real connection point, something we could maybe bond over. And then there was the unexpected compassion and kindness he showed. That was real and uncensored. I did pray for it; I just didn't think it would happen like this and so soon. I wrench my lips to the side as I realize what I had just thought.

"That would be me trying to control your actions, Lord." I sigh long and hard. "Sorry about that again. I'm sure this is your perfect timing, and I just pray that you will be patient with me. Please help me be forgiving toward this man. Help me to see him the way you see him. In your Son's perfect name, amen."

Five

I hear my name being called in the wonderfully southern way that only Michelle Gibson can. She manages to stretch the two syllables of Dixie into at least four. She stands and waves at me from the corner of the café, and every male head in the place turns to watch. She is blonde and tan and absolutely poured into her designer jeans and blouse. I can't help it; my face breaks into a huge grin.

"Hey, Michelle"—I hug her before we sit—"thanks for meeting me."

"I'm so happy you called, sugar!" she beams. "I just hope this is for fun and not something about that cute little cottage you bought."

"Honestly, I just wanted a little girl time. I've either been working away on the cottage or writing music and preparing for the upcoming semester, and I've let two weeks fly by. I felt like it was time to seek out some company." As I said it, I realized it was true. I had so enjoyed our lunch a few weeks earlier that I had wanted a repeat.

"Well, honey, you have come to the right place. I have made girl-time into an art form. My Bob says that if there were degrees in girl-time, I would have a PhD," she says this last with a little head shake, and I can't help it, I giggle.

"Who's Bob?" I ask because I know she's not married.

"He's my boyfriend. He's been my boyfriend on and off for eight years." She rolls her eyes at this. "I've tried other flavors, but Bob is the one." There's a little sadness in her voice this time, and I feel a protectiveness rise up in me.

"What's holding him up? You are fantastic. Any man would be a fool not to snatch you up!" I say, and she smiles a big giant smile.

"You're so sweet, Dixie." She looks over at me and breathes in deep and says the one thing I never expected. "You see, Bob is blind. His hold up is that he doesn't think that life with a blind man would be the happy ending I deserve."

The irony of the situation just about does me in. I am sitting across the table from a woman who looks like an angel. Several men in this café will have sore necks tonight from having craned their heads to stare at her. And she is in love with a blind man. It's perfect, absolutely perfect. It means he understands the part of her that I fell for as well. The guileless part that wears her emotions on her sleeve would be what he *sees* in her. And on her part, it means that she knows that he loves her for everything other than the parts other men want her for.

"Oh, Michelle, I liked you before, but now I think you are about the best person I ever met." She lights up as she realizes that I understand. "You just stick with it. He'll come around. I've known you five seconds, and I understand that you're the type of woman that always gets what she wants."

The rest of lunch goes by quickly during which I manage to drop the fact that I am having JOB build my furniture and my doors.

"Ooooh, Dixie! That place is amazing. Did you know that the owner is the brother of Mason McCoy? I even heard that Mason works there with Johnny when he's in town." At the look on my face, she pauses. "Don't tell me you don't know who Mason McCoy is! My goodness, Dixie, I know you said you used to work shut away in a subterranean lab, but come on!"

"Yes, of course, I've heard of him. He's on that popular TV show about the shipwrecked people. I met him yesterday actually. He was at the shop. Seems like a decent guy." Even to my own ears, I manage to sound casual.

"I think so too. I sold his bungalow to him, and he was very nice. At first I thought he was being all 'I'm a big shot Hollywood guy so keep your distance' cold, because he was very quiet. I mean, don't get me wrong; he was polite, but I think that he's kind of a sad guy." She sighs and looks toward the ceiling as she visits her memories "I guess it could have been an act, you know, kind of James Dean moody, but for some reason, I don't think so. He never once hit on me, and he didn't underestimate me. I liked him."

I feel a small chink fall away. Just a small one though. My new-found best friend has great judgment, but it's not based on all the facts. I know a couple that are horrifying.

I walk Michelle to her car and tell her that I had a great time. She hugs me and leans back to look at me while grasping my upper arms.

"I've got a showing Saturday morning at 9 a.m. and a closing at 11 a.m., but I'm free the rest of the day. What do you say we go on over to the Red Lily for some good old fashion pampering? I'm talking the works— manicure, pedicure, massage, and um, maybe we could even get you a haircut?" Her eyebrows arch on this last word, and she bites her lip. She looks so worried that she's hurt my feelings that it makes me laugh.

My hair...where do I begin? It's a giant mass of tangles that some people call natural curls. Thick is an understatement; I have to use newspaper rubber bands to hold my braid in place. The color is the one good thing; it is a deep, dark, and shiny mahogany. Most days, I wear it in one or two thick braids or a high ponytail such as now.

"Um, sure, we could do that, Michelle. If you don't think the barber will run screaming the second she sees me!"

"Honey, the fact that you use the term *barber* explains everything."

Then she hugs me again and says she will pick me up at my place Saturday at noon. As I climb onto my bike and ride toward home, I feel genuinely happy. I praise God for this change and am rewarded with big, fat tears streaming down my ridiculously grinning face.

Six

L ater that afternoon, just as I finished potting the last geranium for the newly finished sleeping porch, my cell phone starts playing the first few notes of "Jet City Woman." I don't recognize the number, but it's a local area code so I answer.

"Dixie Bryan speaking."

"Hello, Miss Bryan. This is Mason McCoy. We met yesterday morning at my brother's store?" He sounds a bit unsure of himself. And why is he calling me? Shouldn't it be a carpenter or his brother?

"I remember, Mr. McCoy. Are you calling to schedule a time for someone to come by for those measurements?"

"Actually, I was wondering if I could come by and take them down this afternoon or tomorrow morning. My brother is out of town with his wife for their anniversary, and I'm running the show for them."

What! Oh dear. Him in my house? *Lord, give me strength.*

"You actually work there then?"

"Ms. Bryan, are you scared that I'm going to screw this up?"

"No. Well, maybe a little." He laughs out loud at this admission, and I move to explain myself. "It's just that I know you're an actor, so I'm a bit surprised you do this as well."

"There's lots of down time in acting, so I pitch in and help during those times. My brother—Johnny—and I learned carpentry from our Dad. We spent lots of time as kids in his woodshop."

"Okay then. Well, come on by today if you can. I have plans tomorrow."

After we hang up, I wonder for a moment at the direction this is heading. Isn't this what I have been praying about? Is this God saying "put up or shut up"? I have to be open-minded and look at Mason McCoy as a child of God not the monster that caused the biggest tragedy of my life. Can I do it? One thing I know for sure: if I can't, I am doomed.

I walk into the bathroom and wash my hands and my face. When I finish, I stand and look at myself in the mirror. My already olive-toned skin has taken on a deeper glow from the jogging and bike riding I've been able to do. My tall frame was already toned but now I am showing muscle definition in my arms and legs. I'm not a beautiful woman by any stretch of the imagination, but I am very unusual looking. My husband used to say I was sexy, but then he was drunk much of the time. I do have a good strong jaw line and high cheekbones, but my bottom lip sticks out too far and my eyes turn down on the inside corners the way a cat's eyes do. I have a high forehead, causing me to always have to have bangs even when they are out of fashion. And my hair, well I've been down that road. Ugghhh. I mean, really. I do love the color of my hair, and the shade of my eyes is something I have always been secretly proud of. They are a deep vibrant emerald green. I have a diverse stew of genetics from Irish and Scottish to Mulatto and Native American. They all add up to my very unusual coloring and bone structure. I look into the mirror and take a deep breath and reach up and undo the long braids and run a wide-tooth comb through the locks. The braids have actually managed to create looser waves in the mass of curls, and on impulse, I decide to leave it down.

Walking out into the kitchen area, I open a bottle of Dry Creek Meritage and pour it into a decanter for later that evening. Then I take out some vegetables and begin cutting them up for some kebobs. Just as I'm wrapping the tray up and sticking it in the fridge, there is a knock on the front door.

I smooth my hands over my hair, breathe out through my nose, and send up a quick prayer again. As I walk over to the glass and screen front door, I can see him peering in, and he has a wistful, somewhat nostalgic look on his face. I wonder if this is a look tied to love of the work he and his brother do.

"Hi," I say as I open the door and invite him in. "Welcome."

He looks at me and almost seems startled by my presence. Whoa, this dude really gets into his work, or maybe he had a nip of something on the way over. I guess my puzzlement shows on my face because suddenly he smiles.

"Hello, Miss Bryan. Thank you for being so accommodating. You look great by the way. I love your hair down like that." As he says this his eyes first widen then narrow as they move from my hair all the way down to my feet. "You actually make cutoff sweatpants look good." There's the smirk.

How can he do that? I feel such conflicting emotions, but the overwhelming one right now is desire. How does this make any sense at all? I mean I know the saying is that love and hate are two sides of the same coin, but I never really believed that. This is getting really irritating.

"Um…thank you? Anyway, let me show you around a little so you can get a feel for my style, and then you can get your measurements."

I lead him up the stairs first because I want to get the personal area done with. This loft is going to be my sleeping area—the place I want to put the custom-made king size bed. There is an amazing view here through the wall of windows above the front porch roof, and I plan to wake up to it every morning.

"This loft is where I want to put a king-size bed. I would like for it to be right in the middle of the space with four big meaty posts. No footboard to block the view of the ocean but a great headboard that I can pile tons of pillows against." I stop at this point and look over at him to see if he is following me. He is making marks in a small notebook, and he looks up as I quit speaking. He gives a quick little smile and walks around the loft, stepping off the space. He looks into the bathroom and opens a few doors.

"What about a closet? There's not one up here. Do you need an armoire built as well?" he asks.

"Actually, I was thinking about putting a window seat under this dormer. I can make it extend down the wall on either side and put drawers in. I only wear articles of clothing that can be folded up other than the occasional jacket or dress and those can be hung in one of the downstairs bedroom closets."

"I really like that idea, Miss Bryan. We could build that for you as well out of the same material as the bed."

"Look, I think we are beyond *miss*. Please call me Dixie. And I would very much like you to include the window seat in your proposal drawings."

He grins at me before looking back down at his notepad. It makes him look like a young boy, and I am momentarily shaken. After a couple more circuits of the room, he looks up and says, "Next?"

We head down the stairs, and I lead him to the right side of the cottage where there is a fireplace, two sofas, and behind them my custom-built dove-gray baby grand piano. Hanging on the wall behind it is a Goldblatt violin and De Grassi guitar. It is my favorite corner of the house.

"I would like to have a desk built here under this window. Nothing too deep, just enough to sit at and transfer my compositions from sheet music to Noteflight, an online program."

This time, he pulls out his measuring tape and measures the area under the window. As I watch him, I am somewhat amused at the fact that about ten million teenage girls would give their right arms to be standing where I am right now. When he is finished writing down his measurements, he turns and looks at me with raised eyebrows. "What next, Dixie?"

"Just down this short hallway please. Follow me."

"With pleasure, Dixie." He drawls out my name like a southern prayer. Oh my goodness, he is flirting with me now.

I stop in the hallway that leads to three doors—one at the end of the hall that leads out onto the sleeping porch, one to the left, and one to the right that each lead to decent-sized bedrooms. In the hallway to the right, there's also an alcove that contains the washer and dryer. Currently, this is covered with a shower curtain. This is where I lead him.

"My vision here, Mr. McCoy, is to install a large sliding door to cover this alcove when not in use. I would like to have the upper and lower brackets to be made from repurposed wrought iron, and in a perfect world, the door will be an old barn door."

"Dixie, please, call me Mason. And let me say that I love your vision. You have great taste. I just hope my brother and I can make it come to life." His words have no sarcasm to them at all. I feel like he truly means this, and I feel yet another small chink fall away. It's a great feeling.

"Thank you, Mason." I say with a smile. "Anything else you need while you're here?"

"Actually, I was hoping to ask for a favor from you." He pauses and suddenly seems shy and unsure of himself. He swallows and looks directly in my eyes.

"You see, this cottage used to belong to my grandmother when I was a young boy. I spent many nights here during the summer with my brother and sister..." he pauses, and when he looks at me there is pain, as well as hope in his eyes. I am stunned, and yet, it makes sense of some of his behavior when he first arrived. I nod my head at him to indicate he should ask whatever it is he wants. I see his shoulders relax, and he goes on,

"Obviously, the interior has been gutted and remodeled and looks very little like it used to." He looks back toward the living area as he says this.

"However, we used to sleep on the back porch most nights. Granma would put a fan out there, and we would act like we were camping. It was a great time in my life. I would like to see it if it's okay with you."

I can see from his face that it was, and I'm suddenly very nervous about showing the porch to him. It's the one part of the house that I have completely redone. Oh well, what's done is done.

I lead him down the hallway and to the 1920s-era Dutch-style door. I have restored it by sanding it and staining it a deep walnut to match the floors. He must recognize it because his eyes widen slightly. Then I open the door and step out into my own personal wonderland. Behind me, I hear him gasp.

Seven

"Are you okay, Mr. McCoy?"

His eyes are wide and round as he looks around the large sun porch. The room is twelve feet deep and runs the length of the house. Directly across from the door to the house is a glass door leading to the backyard. I have scraped and refinished the floors to a gleaming whitewashed wood. The wall all the way around is thirty-six-inch tall and made from round rock that I painted white from the inside. The columns leading up to the ceiling are thick and square in perfect juxtaposition to the round rocks. The spaces in between are screened in but also covered with large slat blinds to help protect against the afternoon sun. Running all the way around from the roof to the floor, I have hung beautiful white outdoor curtains that flutter in the early evening breeze. There are three black ceiling fans spinning lazily, helping keep the whole porch cool. To the left, on the west end, is a seating area where I have utilized the rocking chairs and porch swing I found stored here when I purchased the place. Each has been restored, the wicker on the rocking chairs restrung, and the beautifully carved and curved wood re-stained. The porch swing is wide and deep and solid. Everywhere, there are accents of red gingham, damask and toile, and pots of red geraniums and teacup roses. But the very best thing about the porch is on the right side—a swinging porch bed.

Mason's mouth is hanging open as he looks at it. I have hung thick steel chains from the ceiling and attached them to a metal bed frame that I found on the porch. It is sturdy wrought iron and has the most wonderful ornate design on the headboard. I searched the local antique shops and found two small twin beds with similar headboards and welded them to the sides, creating a three-sided cocoon after filling it in with a custom-sized therapeutic mattress and tons of pillows.

"This is where I have been sleeping the past few nights. It's much better than the couch." For some reason, I say this in a half whisper.

He turns and looks at me and his normally sky-blue eyes have darkened into a color closer to violet. He looks at me in a way that makes my heart thump instead of beat. Oh my, what the heck is this all about?

"That"—he gulps and seems to be at a loss for words for a second—"is absolutely the most amazing thing I have ever seen, Miss Bryan. Did I say I was impressed with your imagination? Understatement." His voice is about a half octave lower than usual.

I drag my gaze from his and look at the bed and around the sleeping porch and back to him. In those few seconds, his face has come back to normal, and he is smiling the lopsided smile that has helped make him famous.

"I must confess that I am stunned at what you have done with this space. This was my granma's favorite part of the house, and red was her favorite color as well." He turns around, taking in all the elements of the room. He stopped on the rocking chairs and looked back at me with an unasked question on his lips.

"I found those here and refinished them. Same with the porch swing and the bed frame." I told him and gestured to each.

"I remember them. I can't believe they were still here. There was at least one owner between Granma and you."

"They were piled under a tarp over to one side. This whole porch was in really bad shape. I think the last owner spent the bulk of their remodeling effort on the front porch and interior."

"Did you do this all yourself?"

"Yes. I did actually. It wasn't too bad, just a lot of elbow grease and time with a paintbrush." For some reason, I am blushing under his praise. It really ticks me off.

"But how did you manage the new posts and the bed? I'm surprised the roof was structurally sound enough."

"Actually, Mason, this cottage is as solid as they come. One of the reasons I bought it was the craftsmanship." I look up at the roof as I recall crawling around in the attic and anchoring the brackets.

"As for how I did all that, well, let's just say in my former life, I spent a lot of time around engineers. I picked up a few pointers on how to maneuver and manipulate small equipment to create big changes."

Our eyes collide, and he looks as if he is about to say more but doesn't. Instead, I ask him, "Was it your grandparents that installed the Japanese gardens in the backyard?"

I walk past him and open the back door and step onto the decking walkway. The backyard was a close second to the sleeping porch as to why I chose this cottage. The garden is laid out in the paradise-garden style with the walkways winding through walls of bamboo, azalea bushes, cedar, and willow trees. At the end of the walkway, a bridge leads over the lotus pond to a platform containing a beautifully weathered teak Buddha statue. Everything is overgrown and in need of manicuring, and the decking needs to be treated, and the pond should be restocked with some koi fish, but the original designer of the garden did such a beautiful job that it will be easy to bring it back to glory.

"My great-grandfather was stationed in Japan during WWII. He met my great-grandmother there, and they married. She was Japanese." He smiles and reaches out to pull a flower off the nearest Azalea bush. As he twirls it around, he continues, "My granma was born there and was in high school before they moved back here after her mother died. She said that her father created this garden in her mother's honor." There is emotion, raw and real, in his voice, and I feel so much that I was not expecting that I am momentarily dizzy. I grab the railing and lean against it.

"Mason," I start, and he looks over at me. I am momentarily struck mute by how beautiful he is. It's as if he walked out of a medieval-era painting with his classic Eurasian looks. Just as the silence becomes weird, I ask, "Would you care for a glass of wine? I have a bottle decanting in the kitchen, and if you have the time, I would love to hear some stories about this house."

"You know what, Dixie? That sounds like my idea of a great time. I just need to make a quick phone call, and I'll join you in the kitchen shortly."

As I walk back down the walkway, I hear the buttons on the phone and just before I enter the sleep porch I hear him say, "Hey, sweetheart."

Eight

When he walks back in, I'm turning the kebobs on the hibachi-style grill and have two glasses of the deep red wine sitting on the counter. He sits on one of the barstools and picks up a glass.

"Are you hungry?" I ask.

"I wasn't, but smelling those, I am suddenly ravenous." He smiles at me, but he looks at the kebobs, and I believe that he is speaking of the food. I have a salad in the fridge and some rolls in the oven. He was on the phone for several minutes.

"I hope you don't mind. I figured if we were going to drink some wine, we should have something in our bellies." I didn't look at him. Instead, I concentrated on turning the skewers containing the prime cut filet mignon. Suddenly, a thought strikes me. "You're not a vegetarian, are you?"

He chuckles. "No, I may be part of Hollywood now, but I was raised in Louisiana, and I appreciate a good cut of beef."

"Well, Hollywood, there's hope for you yet."

"Glad you have faith in me." He sips his wine and murmurs appreciatively. "Why don't you tell me about yourself, Dixie? Where are you from?"

Oh man. I hadn't really thought this far ahead. It's not in my nature to lie, so I just play it evasively.

"Well, I grew up in Arkansas, went to college, and got a job right after school, but I decided on a career change, and that's what brought me here." I say this, hoping it is so boring he will move on. No such luck.

"Let me guess, you were"—he looks at me thoughtfully before continuing—"in the band. No, wait, chess club." I snort and throw a dish rag at him. "Okay, it must have been future business leaders club."

"None of the above actually. I wasn't much of a club or group joiner." I decide to try and divert him. "Now, the reason why I'm feeding you such amazing wine and food is so you will fill me in on the history of my cottage. Get to spilling."

Nine

A few hours later, I am walking Mason McCoy to my front door. Somehow it is approaching 10 p.m., and I have just spent the better part of a Friday night with a man that has haunted my nightmares for months, and it was pleasant. I am amazed anew at the ability of God to completely eradicate my preconceived expectations.

On the front porch, Mason turns and takes my right hand and lifts it to his lips. Those lips are full and so soft I can barely feel them on my skin. When he lifts his eyes to mine, they are sparkling with mischief and amusement.

"Miss Dixie Bryan, I have had a very enjoyable evening and much unexpected. It's not very often I spend an entire day talking with someone who isn't the slightest bit interested in talking about my day job. I will be back in touch with the drawings." He pauses and looks me in the eye. "I really hope to continue the friendship I feel we've started here. We seem to have a good connection, and I get the feeling we have only scratched the surface."

I smile back at him. "I think we can make a stab at that. I only have one other friend here in Bay St. Louis, so who am I to turn down another one?"

I stand in my door and watch him walk down the deck walkway to his jeep. I clear my mind and put off any judgments regarding tonight. I am going to nurse this relationship and work toward the forgiveness I need to reach with Mr. Mason McCoy. I don't know if I will ever come clean with him about my identity and what happened in the past, and I don't know if it matters, but with my growing connection to this town, I feel like it may be inevitable. Turning back toward the interior of the house, I sigh loudly and decide I will deal with that situation when it presents itself.

As I sit down at my piano and begin to play one of Mozart's piano sonatas, I close my eyes and lose myself in the rise and fall of notes and do my best to not think about Mason's famously beautiful blue eyes, ebony hair, and slight bowed legs.

Ten

The next afternoon, I find myself sitting in a black swivel chair in front of a giant mirror with a look of intense fear on my face. The blissful relaxation that the hour massage followed by a manicure and pedicure brought evaporated the instant I saw Jean-Luc, holding the black cape like a matador. I look over at Michelle, and she giggles at me. I don't know which is scaring me the most—the look of complete horror on Jean-Luc's face or the canary yellow, asymmetrical Mohawk on his head. I know my hair is far from stylish but really?

"Sit, sit!" he directs me. He pulls my hair out of the braid and begins running his fingers through the tangles and fluffs it all up and out. "Girl, you have come to the right place. Jean-Luc will take care of you. Jean-Luc will tame this giant mess into something so beautiful it will make you weep with joy!" He seems almost giddy with the idea of such a challenge.

Michelle comes over and puts her head next to mine. "Don't worry, Dixie, please. Jean-Luc is a magician with scissors. I trust him implicitly, or I would never have brought you to him." Then she turned to my cockatoo-crowned friend. "Jean-Luc, do your stuff, but do not touch the color." There is a momentary look of mutiny on his face, but she puts up an elegant, manicured hand.

"No! Even you couldn't improve upon what she was born with, my dear Jean-Luc." With that, she puts a hand on his lips to stifle any protest and sashays over to a large zebra-striped coach and has a seat. Even a gay man like Jean-Luc is visibly affected by the beauty that is Michelle Gibson. He gives himself a little shake and begins the symphony of snips.

Forty-five minutes later, I am dried and styled, and I can barely believe the woman in the mirror is me. My bangs are full and artful, and the layering and thinning that Jean-Luc skillfully applied have created the illusion of cascading waves that end just below my shoulder blades. He's shown me how to use a large round brush to achieve the same affect on my own although I am not very confident in my own abilities.

"Oh my," Michelle breathes when she walks up. "Jean-Luc, *mmm, mmm, mmm.* You have outdone yourself this time!" He blushes under the praise, and I am thinking of his face when he sees the ginormous tip I am about to leave him.

On the way home, Michelle convinces me to go out with her and Bob that night. "No way am I letting you waste that hair on eating alone." *Besides*, I tell myself, *I am anxious to meet Bob, and she's right, I have been spending enough time alone.*

Eleven

I arrive first to a small Italian bistro in the Old Town district. I choose an outdoor table so we can enjoy the mild breeze coming from the waterfront. Even though we are approaching Halloween, the temperatures are still in the low eighties and very comfortable. Breaking with tradition, I order a glass of Jameson Gold on the rocks. I did walk here after all. My beautiful new hairdo is working its magic and two different men approach the table and ask to join me, forcing me to explain that I am waiting for friends.

When I spot Michelle and Bob, they are walking hand in hand up the wooden ramp to the deck where I am sitting. Bob has a very slim silver cane that lightly taps the ground in front of him. His eyes are wrapped in dark sunglasses, and his light brown hair flops over his forehead. He has lush lips and a strong bone structure. He looks like he works out and takes very good care of himself. My first thought when I look at him is that he is an attractive man, but when I see the adoration in Michelle's eyes, it makes him downright gorgeous.

I stand as they approach and greet them both, and Bob smiles at me and says, "With a name like Dixie, I was expecting someone from the deep south, but your accent has traces of Arkansas, Mississippi Delta, and let's see Massachusetts? That's quite a mix!" And he seems delighted by the surprising medley of my voice tones.

"You are good, Bob. I was born in Arkansas, went to school in New Hampshire and Massachusetts, and then worked in and around Memphis for years."

"He has such a gift for that kind of thing. I swear that's why he likes living here. The tourists provide an unending supply of audible entertainment for him." Michelle laughs as she and Bob sit down, and the waiter approaches to take their drink order.

"So, Dixie, Michelle tells me you bought the old Brennan place on Sycamore?" Bob asks.

Brennan—that must be Mason's grandmother's maiden name or maybe her married name. Perhaps Bob will be able to fill me in. "Yes, I suppose I did. I am absolutely enchanted with it too."

"She's been working like a madwoman on it, Bob. She has totally redone the sleeping porch, and it is like a fairy tale come true." I notice that as Michelle is talking, she is constantly touching him whether it's his hand, arm, leg, or face. He is completely relaxed with these touches too, and it seems he orients himself around them. "Oh, and guess who she is having build some furniture for her?"

Bob turns his head toward me. "Judging by the excitement in Michelle's voice, I'm going to guess the infamous McCoy brothers?"

"Yes, actually. I stumbled upon their store one morning while jogging and fell in love with the work. They're going to custom-build a bed and desk for me and also install a window seat in my loft and some sliding barn doors for my washer/dryer alcove. I'm expecting a call in the next couple days with the renderings so they can get started."

"Tell Bob who came to your house to take the measurements." Michelle is like a little girl with a secret. She is shifting in her seat and practically bouncing. Bob reaches over and pats her hand and grins at her. She visibly melts and sighs.

"I've deduced the answer just from how you are bouncing in your seat, sugar." He turns his head back toward me. "What did you think of our local celebrity, Mason McCoy?"

"He was really insightful and understood the goals I had for the cottage. Of course, it was probably fueled by the fact that he spent so much time there as a child and knew a lot of the history."

"I'm impressed that he told you about the cottage. In fact, I'm very surprised that Mason made a house call." Bob puts his finger over his lips, and I feel sure that he is about to say more, but he doesn't.

Michelle picks up the lull. "I think it was a little more than that. He stayed for dinner and everything. I think Mason is intrigued by our Miss Dixie. And why wouldn't he be? She's only thirty-one years old and has like three or four degrees, has lived all over, has this mysterious air to her, and if you could just see her, Bob, you would understand. She's amazing looking."

"It's actually five degrees, thank you very much," I say in my best Elvis drawl. "But I am only amazing looking, if by amazing you mean in the *weird* category. Although I must say Jean-Luc did a magician's job on my hair."

Bob perks up. "What are your degrees in, Dixie? I hope you don't mind me asking. It's just that I am a bit of an academician myself." Michelle had told me that Bob teaches world history and advanced classes in Civil War and Revolutionary America.

"I have two PhDs. One in quantum physics and one in biogeochemistry; two masters. One in music performance and one in plant biology. Last, but not least, I have a degree in basket weaving." After a beat, they both start laughing. "No, really, I have a bachelor's in musical composition."

"Well, Dixie, you're quite the slacker, aren't you? Good to hear you are finally gonna do something with your life here in Bay St. Louis," Bob says so drily and straight-faced that Michelle and I just fall out laughing.

Over the most delicious crawfish ravioli and crusty rolls, I tell Michelle and Bob stories about being an eighteen-year-old double doctorate student at MIT in Boston. Bob is such a history buff that he peppers me with question after question about the historical sites there. I am thrilled with the opportunity to talk about those days and have someone truly understand the profound respect I felt for the past while walking the same streets that historical figures such as Ben Franklin, Sam Adams, and Patrick Henry walked two centuries before.

"Thank you for persevering through my questions, Dixie. Of course, I have read many accounts of the

Revolutionary period, but to get a first-hand account of the area is priceless."

"You really should visit yourself, Bob. Every history buff should make a pilgrimage to Boston, Philly, and Gettysburg at the minimum. There are walking tours where you could wear headphones that play a soundtrack that makes you feel as though you were there."

Michelle squeezes Bob's hand and says, "We should plan it, honey."

"That's nice of you, sugar, but I know war history bores you to death."

I see a brief flash of pain cross her face, and I raise my eyebrows at her, encouraging her to speak up.

"Not really, Bob, I just don't know much about it. If you would help me to understand and explain everything, I think I would love it. Besides, as long as I am with you, I'm happy."

He turns his head toward her, and at first, I think he's going to argue. Instead he lifts her hand to his lips. "I've been unfair to you by assuming what you would and wouldn't like, haven't I?"

"It doesn't matter, love. It's never too late to start listening to me." She is smiling, but I see the tears in her eyes. "Besides, even if I didn't like it, there's bound to be awesome shopping in Boston." That was the charm of Michelle; she can lighten any mood.

Just about the time I am sending my credit card with the waiter, Michelle sucks in her breath, and I turn to look in the direction she is looking. I see Mason McCoy and a very beautiful, very young woman walking toward our table. The hostess is guiding him to the setting directly behind ours, and he makes eye contact with me from several feet away. My heart skips a beat, and he bumps into an empty seat at the same time. As his date stops to look back at him, he touches her arm to stop her.

"Hello, Miss Bryan. Michelle, Bob, good to see you two." He smiles at both and kisses Michelle on her cheek and touches Bob's shoulder. He smiles a sweet smile and inclines his head in my direction. Then he turns and looks at his date.

"This is Hanna, my co-star on *Shipwrecked*. Hanna, Michelle here sold my house to me, and Bob and I went to school together. He's one of my oldest friends here." He smiles easily and warmly at Bob, and I tuck this little bit of information away. Then he turns toward me, and our eyes make contact, and I watch him take in my new hairstyle, the touch of make up, and the simple summer dress I have on.

"And this is Dixie Bryan, the one I was telling you about. She bought my grandmother's old cottage. Johnny and I are going to do some custom pieces for her."

Hanna smiles the easy smile of a woman who knows she is more beautiful than all the other women in the room and feels somewhat sorry for the rest of us mere mortals. She has very long, light brown hair that has beautiful blonde highlights. Her eyes are a deep brown and huge. She is also petite and has to look up at Mason.

"Oh yes, Mason told me about how nice it was to see the little house he spent so much of his childhood in." I watch her eyes flit over my face, hair, and body and find me lacking. "I hear from Sandra that you're taking over the music dept at the high school this winter, as well."

What? Wait, who's Sandra, and why was she talking to this girl and Mason about my job at the high school. The confusion must have shown on my face because Michelle explains, "Mason's brother Johnny is married to Sandra King, the principal of BSL High School. She's always used her maiden name for work."

I am stunned for a moment but am able to smile and nod as if this makes complete and perfect sense. I know that Hanna's dropped this bit of information as a territorial move to let me and Michelle know that she is serious enough with Mason to be having conversations with his family, but still, I am shaken that I was a topic of conversation with the McCoy family. Not good, not good at all.

The waiter returns with my black AMEX card and receipt for dinner, which I sign quickly and stand to leave. Michelle is looking at me with a big question mark hanging in the air between us but recovers quickly and moves to stand and Bob follows.

"I have your drawings and proposal ready by the way." Mason says, and I realize that with my heeled sandals, he has to look slightly up at me. I know he has noticed, as well, because a slight frown crosses his face. "Would you care to meet with Johnny and me Monday at the shop? Say around eight-thirty, just before he opens?"

"Sure, sure, that'll work fine. I'm looking forward to meeting Johnny and getting the project started." I look down at the table and realize there is about one-fourth of my drink left and feel a momentary thankfulness that is enormous. I pick it up and drain the glass in one swallow and flip my hair over my shoulder the way I have seen Michelle do several times. Mason's eyes widen slightly, and as I walk away, I hear him ask the waiter for one of whatever I had been drinking.

Twelve

Sunday morning, I ride my bicycle over to a small church I had spotted in the neighborhood. It was covered with white clapboard siding and had an old-fashioned steeple and bell. As I park my bike in the shade of an ancient Magnolia tree and take my bible out of the front basket, I see the pastor at the front door greeting the parishioners as they enter. This is something you don't see much of these days. I queue up in line, and I feel the normal glances as people try and figure out who I am and who I might be visiting with.

"Good morning, miss. I'm Reverend White." I can't help it. I blink a little, and he chuckles because I am sure he's used to people being stunned at the irony of a black man with the deepest ebony skin you have ever seen having the surname *White*. "Are you visiting with someone this morning, miss?"

"Oh, Bryan—Dixie Bryan, and no, I just moved here to Bay St. Louis and am looking for a church."

He smiles an amazingly kind smile and puts a hand on my shoulder and says, "I hope you find what you're looking for here at Main Street church, Miss Bryan. We would be proud to have you."

His deep voice and kind eyes are just so fatherly that I'm blinking back tears as I walk inside. This is what I need—a place to let go and let God in and not worry about the world outside. I feel my spirit jumping for joy inside as we launch into rousing renditions of "I'll Fly Away", "It Is Well", and "Old Rugged Cross." The families around me welcome me and hold my hand during the prayers, and at the end of service, one of the older women drags me by the hand up to a young woman I saw leading the choir.

"Nell, this girl needs to be singing in the choir!" she says. I think her name was Sally. I look down at her and immediately panic.

"Oh no, this is my first visit. I'm new to the area. The choir looks full." I look from face-to-face, and they are both just staring at me. Nell looks from me to Ms. Sally and back.

"You sure, Ms. Sally?"

"What'd'ya mean, 'Am I sure'? I stood next to this girl the whole service, and she got it. Sounds like mix up of Ella, Etta, and Koko all in a skinny white girl." At this praise, both I and Nell take a step back and gape at Ms. Sally. Nell then looks over at me and holds out her hand.

"Well, if Ms. Sally Charles says you're that good, I will take her word. We practice this afternoon from four-thirty to five-thirty. Can you be here?" She still looks a little skeptical, but she is friendly, and I know this is more about her willingness to indulge Ms. Sally than wanting another body in the choir. But I miss singing with Giles and the guys so much, and I think this will help fill that void.

"Yes, I'll be here. Thank you for taking a chance on me, Nell."

Thirteen

I'm napping on the porch bed that afternoon when my cell phone goes off. It takes a few seconds before I am fully awake and able to answer.

"Hello?" I groan.

"Dixie, did I wake you?" says a male voice straight out of my nightmares/ dreams.

"Yes, actually you did." I say, feeling a little truculent.

"Were you sleeping on the porch bed?" he says, and his voice has taken on a thickness that is primal. I sit straight up and run my hand through my hair. The movement has caused the bed to sway slightly, and I feel my eyes get heavy again.

"Yes, Mason, I was." I clear my throat because my own voice is deeper with sleep. "It's a great afternoon for it with the cooler temperatures."

There is silence for a few seconds and just as I am about to ask if he "can hear me now" he says, "I was calling to see if I could stop by and bring those renderings. I've found myself with some free time and can think of nothing better than spending it with a friend, talking about building stuff."

He's light and cheerful as he says this, and I find myself actually looking forward to it. After all, Friday night was a lot of fun.

"What time were you thinking?" I ask.

"About five o'clock? That's an hour." he says.

Oh crap. Choir practice is in half an hour. "No, Mason, I'm sorry. I have plans and won't be home then."

"Oh. Well, another time then," he says, and he sounds so hurt it almost makes me laugh. Mr. Hollywood isn't used to be turned down.

"Well, if you can wait until five forty-five, I'll be home. I have choir practice until five thirty just down the street."

"You sing in a choir? As in a church choir?" I am somewhat offended at how surprised he sounds.

"Well, as of today. I just joined the Main Street Church choir. It's my first practice." I am aware that I sound petulant.

"Uh, Dixie, Main Street is a mostly black church."

"I'm fully aware, Mason. And your point is?" I can't help it, my voice has gone icy.

"Whoa, whoa there, Miss Bryan. Before you go getting your undies in a bind, I'm not being racist; I'm just trying to imagine you singing in that style of choir." Here he stops and giggles just a bit. "I can wait on you to get back from choir practice, Dixie Bryan. What kind of heathen would I be if I got in the way of that?"

After I hang up, I scramble into the guest bedroom and pull off the pajama pants I had on and pull on a sundress and cardigan over my camisole. I have ten minutes to get to the church, so I don't take the time to freshen up, I just jump on my bike and pedal the six blocks over to the church.

Fourteen

It's 5:42 p.m. when I pull back up at my house and stow my bike just inside the privacy fence gate. Mason is sitting in one of the wicker barrel chairs on my front porch. He has a brown V-neck T-shirt on with his faded jeans and rope sandals. On the ground between his feet is a reusable grocery bag. He smiles lazily at me as I walk around the ancient tree to where he's sitting.

"There's the songbird. How was church?" he asks.

"Well, they didn't kick me out, so I would say round one is a success." I walk by him and unlock the door and keep going, knowing that he will follow me in.

"I took a chance on the fact that you wouldn't have had supper yet."

He sets the bag on the large kitchen island and starts pulling items out—a large loaf of crusty French bread, a brown box containing fried crawfish tails, and other smaller containers of lettuce, cheese, and a special sauce. Finally, a bottle of Joel Gott's 2009 Zinfandel comes out of the bag, and I can't help but smile.

"I hope you like po'boys?" he says as he puts the sauce, lettuce, and crawfish in a paper bag and starts shaking. I am distracted by the sight of his biceps flexing as he shakes the bag, but I manage to nod as I begin opening the bottle of wine. He asks for a cookie sheet as he cuts the French bread first in two and then slits it open to create a bed for the crawfish concoction. These he puts into the oven and then turns around and leans back against the counter with his wineglass.

"I like what you've done with your hair." I feel his eyes move over my face and hair. It's messy from the bike ride, but the true testament of Jean-Luc's artistry is that I can run my hand through my hair and restore it to some semblance of order.

"Thank you." I simply say because I am not sure what else to say.

"I was surprised to see you with Michelle and Bob, but it dawned on me that Michelle probably sold this cottage to you."

"Yes, she did, and I just fell in love with her. We've become great friends." I say with a big smile because when I think of Michelle, I can't help but smile.

"She's a nice girl from what I can tell, and there's no denying that she makes Bob happy. In my book, that makes her on par with Mother Teresa."

Interesting. "Tell me about Bob. How do you know him?"

He begins to speak as he pulls the po'boys out. They smell mouthwateringly good, and I suddenly realize I didn't eat lunch. "My grandparents lived here my whole life, but when I was very young, my parents and siblings and I lived just across the state border in Slidell, Louisiana. When I was a freshman, we moved here permanently, and I was going through an awkward phase." He looks up at me with a wry smile. I pause mid bite and raise my eyebrows.

"What, am I supposed to be surprised? So you were awkward, big deal. I graduated high school at fourteen years old and went to Dartmouth before I could legally drive. I had braces, was so thin, and angular I made Olive Oil look buxom and hair that made the dude from Whitesnake jealous"—by now he's laughing—"so just get over yourself there, Mr. Awkward."

"Okay, okay, Miss Bryan, you've made your point and in an extraordinary manner may I say. So where was I...Ah yes, Bob was my first friend here in Bay St. Louis. He was funny and smart and very popular at school. For some reason, we clicked even though we were complete opposites. I was moody and dark, and he was the eternal optimist." He smiles and shakes his head at some remembered moment then continues, "Our sophomore year, he talked me into joining the theatre group. He said I was so full of drama that it was a perfect fit. He really is who I credit with my current career." I can see the warmth on his face, and it is genuine. Then after a second a dark cloud passes over his features.

"So why haven't you stayed close?" I take a stab in the dark that this is what caused the look. He takes a deep breath and rolls his head around on his shoulders. He looks everywhere but at me, then suddenly, pins me with a direct gaze.

"I moved to Hollywood the week after high school graduation, but I stayed in close contact with him. He was so much help to me in so many ways." He looks over at me and asks, "Have you seen what he can do with picking apart accents?"

"Yes, I have, and it is amazing how accurate he is."

"Well, he would help me with understanding the roles I was auditioning for. He knew everything from how I should craft my accent to historical and geographical accuracies. And he never once asked for anything in return or took credit for my success." He blows out a deep breath, and his face takes on a pained expression.

"I have always been a passionate conservationist even before I knew there was a movement. In Hollywood, there is a lot of pressure to be involved and not question the motives, and because we are insulated and feed off of each other, it's easy to get caught up in the fervor." He's pacing now. "Bob tried to be my voice of reason, tried to make me take a step back, and have more objectiveness. So we had a major disagreement. The final nail was when he told me that I had become so self-involved that I was blind to the effects of my passion. It drove us apart because I just couldn't understand how he didn't feel the same way I did, and at the time, I was being surrounded by people who told me whatever I wanted to hear."

Now he was clenching his fists into his hair, and I could feel the pain there. I have felt that kind of pain. "I began to feel I was superior to him, and I stopped communicating with him. Then one day, the very thing he warned me about happened, and I couldn't talk to him, the one person I really wanted to talk to, because he had been *right*." Now he was resting his head in his hands and twists around to make eye contact. "Do you know what I'm saying here?"

"I do, yes. I know exactly what you are saying. It is the hardest to reach out to someone when you know they are right, and they have every right to say I told you so, but you know they won't. You know they will instead comfort you even if you brought whatever it was on yourself. That's the hardest to accept because it makes you feel disgusted with the person in the mirror." I whisper the last sentence, and Mason reaches over and takes my hand. Our eyes have not broken contact, and we hold it for several more seconds until Mason disappears behind a shimmering wall of tears. I reach for my glass of wine and blink them away.

"I sensed you would understand. I could feel your sadness that first day. I'm guessing that's what brought you here." I keep my head down because to look at him right then would mean losing it completely. Instead, I draw a shuddering breath.

"I want to talk to you more about this. In fact you have no idea how much I would like to bare my soul and hear your horror story. Do you think we will be able to do that someday, Dixie?" he asks earnestly. I look up quickly and let out a long slow breath then lean my head back and stare up at the ceiling for a few seconds.

He speaks again, "I think it would be cleansing to share with someone who so obviously understands the feelings that go with them." As he says this, he has stood up and is standing between my legs at the barstool and is holding my face with both his hands. I know without a doubt that he is going to kiss me, and

I don't care about anything else right now. I watch his face descend to mine and twist slightly to the left in order to lightly place his lips against mine. We breathe in each other's wine-tainted breath for a couple of seconds and then his lips begin a slow movement. I hear our ragged breathing and nothing else until his tongue slips into my mouth and then I hear my own sharp intake of breath. I haven't felt these feelings since those happy days when David was courting me. But even as I think that, I acknowledge that I have never been kissed like this. My mouth is being completely claimed by Mason's lips, breath, and tongue. Every crevice is explored without urgency, and I feel as if this is what I was made for—this kiss. This goes on for an eternity or a nanosecond, I'm not sure as time ceases to matter, but when he withdraws his mouth, I hiccup with the loss.

I slowly realize I am gripping the barstool arms so hard my fingers are nearly numb. I look down at them as if they were alien objects before slowly letting go. With the eye contact broken, I regain some of my senses. When I look back up, we search each others eyes until I break the contact by looking out the window and blinking away the tears that are on my eyelashes. I am feeling so much grief, and I don't understand why.

"I do think there will be a point in the future that we can talk about all of these things, Mason. In fact, I also look forward to it even though I am sure there will be much wailing and gnashing of teeth." We grin small, sad little grins at each other. "And at some point, we will need to talk about what just happened here too, but not just now, okay?" There is a little pleading in my voice on that one because I just can't bear to hear about real life and girlfriends and such. Not when I am glowing on the inside like this.

"Okay, I would be willing to make that compromise with you because I would like to stretch this feeling out as long as possible too." His look is knowing and likely mirrors mine. "But I have one favor to ask, can we do that one more time before we look at the proposal? Just once more and then you go back to being a client, and I go back to being the Hollywood jerk you are tolerating because my brother has a cool business." His tone is joking, but his look is somewhere between hopeful and smoldering.

"I would like nothing more, Hollywood. I'm actually shocked with myself at how much that statement is true"—this time it is him that sucks in his breath— "but you have to promise me that you will stop because I don't know if I can, and if this goes any further than a moment to forget real life and the pain that lurks there and lose ourselves in a stolen moment, then we will end up hating each other. Do you understand me?"

"Yes. Oh yes, Dixie, I understand you perfectly." This time he pulls me into a standing position and wraps his arms around me. "Has anyone ever told you that you are annoyingly tall, Miss Bryan?" he whispers into my mouth. I shiver in response and then his lips are on mine, and our tongues are dancing. I curl my fists up into his hair and pull him tighter to me, eliciting a groan from him, and he reciprocates by moving a hand up to cradle the back of my head. I don't believe that I am deriving so much comfort from this man, a man that I have hated with a white hot passion for many months. Most anger is irrational as is lust. So perhaps this makes perfect sense. Perhaps making out with Mason McCoy in my kitchen after promising to tell him someday about how he'd created such horror in my life is the most logical thing in the whole wide world.

My hands leave his hair and move down to his face, feeling it as if I was a blind woman, and still the kiss goes on. His tongue is running over my teeth, including my ridiculous little fangs that have always embarrassed me, and the feeling is like none other. As I lick the inside of his upper lip, my hands make it to his shoulders. Suddenly, he breaks the kiss. He reaches up and grabs my hands and puts them down at my side. We are both breathing heavily, and I drop down in my barstool. He walks awkwardly into the restroom, and still I don't lift my head. Eventually, I feel him sit next to me, but I don't look over at him right away.

"Thank you for stopping." He looks over at me, and I smirk at him. "It may take me a few days to actually mean that, but you know, thank you."

He grins back at me and pulls a notepad over in front of us.

"Shall we get down to business?" he says, and he sounds calm, and I feel tremendous gratitude toward him for this. We spend the next half hour going through the drawings and prices he has worked up. The renderings are breathtaking, and I get really excited about how amazing the cottage is going to look with them. Before he leaves, I write a check to the company for the materials so they can get started right away.

Mason turns at the door, and for a second, I think he is going to kiss me again. Instead he says, "I bet you'll be glad to get a real bed soon. Are you still sleeping on the porch?"

"Yes, but it's not a hardship, trust me. I love sleeping out there, but it'll eventually get a little too chilly for it."

"Goodnight, Dixie. Sleep well on your swinging bed."

"Goodnight, Mason. Sweet dreams."

He walks backward down the walkway for several steps and then abruptly turns and sprints to his jeep.

That night I have an old nightmare about the day of the waste plant explosion that killed my husband. In my dream I'm strapped to a chair, and Mason is standing in front of me pointing his finger at me and yelling that it's my fault, all the destruction is my fault, all the deaths are my fault, and I must pay. What makes it a nightmare for me is that I can't speak to defend myself, and my frustration mounts until I'm crying so hard I start to hyperventilate. This dream haunted me for months during my recuperation from the bombing that took my baby's life.

It was easy to understand what the nightmare stemmed from; for weeks I was on a respirator in the hospital, unable to communicate or breathe on my own. The TV in the room was on an all-news station that, because of the bombing, was replaying all the details around the plant explosion. Mason was on the screen often, as he was the de facto celebrity spokesperson for all the outraged environmental groups. I couldn't get away from the constant sound bites of him discussing what evil people he felt me and my husband and the plant owner, National Waste, were. I would become so frustrated from not being able to make him understand the reality behind my involvement. My heart rate would spike as the anger built in my over the reckless way this man used his celebrity to speak about things he knew nothing about; recklessness that would lead to impressionable people performing heinous acts of violence for a skewed sense of *justice*.

Waking up from the dream, I'm initially overcome with a blinding fury that has me doubting the sanity of what I'm doing. Knowing I can't solve this on my own and not wanting to lose ground, I crawl out of the bed and onto the porch floor and press my head to the cool wood planks in supplication.

Fifteen

Monday morning I decide to make a trip into New Orleans to take care of some business and check in on the flat. I want to make sure it is well-stocked with necessities as my cousin Tyler and his wife are coming to stay in it for a few days the following week.

Because the temperature is mild and the sun is shining, I decide to take my motorcycle—a rare treat in a part of the country where rain is so frequent. I became a motorcycle enthusiast while I was in my second year of MIT. It was an efficient mode of travel in a city where traffic was such an issue.

My current love is a Ducati Diavel Cromo. It is an amazingly light and yet muscular bike. As I pull out of the driveway and head toward Highway 90, I have to go through the Depot District, and on impulse, I decide to stop in Just Old Barnwood to see if Johnny is there. I haven't met him yet and feel like I should at least shake his hand.

When I walk in the store, the bell above the door rings, and the person behind the counter looks up. I am surprised to see it is a young teenage boy. He looks up, and I see Mason's face under a shock of white blonde hair. He smiles shyly at me and says, "May I help you?"

"I was wondering if Johnny McCoy was here."

"That's my dad. He's in the back, working on some things. Do you need me to get him?" He's looking at me a little curiously like he should know me but can't place me.

"No, please, not necessary. He and your uncle are making some furniture for me, and I was just going to stop in to see, well, just see if there were any last-minute questions." For some reason I am blushing. I feel like a teenage girl who just got caught spying on her boyfriend.

"Oh cool! You're Ms. Bryan, the new music teacher!" he's suddenly around the counter and holding out his hand. "My name's Colton. I'll be in your class and the choir." I shake his hand, and his enthusiasm starts a blossom of warmth in my chest.

"I'm very pleased to meet you, Colton." I say and mean it. He's polite and adorable. I bet the girls beat down his door or more likely these days, burn up his phone with text messages. "Say, why aren't you in school today?" I ask, using my best teacher tone.

"It's Columbus Day, Ms. Bryan," he says and then chuckles. Oh, not very teacherly of me to not know the school calendar.

"Ah. Okay. Can we pretend I didn't just ask that?" Now he laughs even harder. He's cute, and he laughs at lame jokes. Where was this guy when I was an awkward teenage girl? "Well, it's very nice of you to work in the shop on your day off. Your dad must be very proud of you." He blushes a little under my praise.

"Look, I'm headed out of town, so please just tell your dad I stopped by, and if he needs anything to call me."

"I sure will, Ms. Bryan." He walks me to the door, and I am impressed by how well-mannered he is. He opens the door for me and then freezes as he spots the Ducati. "Whoa!" He breathes, and I totally understand. I smile at him and nod in agreement.

"I know, right? She's as sweet to ride as she is to look at." I put my helmet on, swing my black leather jacket on, and sit on the back of the chrome and black beauty. I give Colton a thumbs up, hit the ignition switch, and pull off. I know that within a couple of hours, the new music teacher will be the talk of his friends, and the story will eventually include me leaving a wall of smoke as I pull a wheelie down Blaize Avenue. The thought makes me giggle for a couple blocks.

Sixteen

At 6 p.m., I let myself into the flat, drop my keys and helmet on the entry table, and make my way over to the refrigerator. My mind is still working through all the minutia of the transactions Mr. Marshall walked me through. I am very pleased with the progress on a charity trust I set up called *Acts 35*, which provides free daycare to low- income working mothers in three different cities, staffed by high-quality certified teachers. The charity also gives funds out to a variety of food banks and shelters. I was not as pleased, however, with some of the letters that Mr. Marshall had for me from some of my deceased husband's family members. I was not surprised at the continuing efforts on their part to profit from me, but I was surprised at how upset I could continue to be by their malicious words. The hurdle I needed to get over with David's family was not being able to understand their greed. They were an upper middle-class family, and David had never wanted for anything, but years earlier when a scientific discovery suddenly made me wealthier than I even knew a person could be, David's mother began using the term *my daughter* instead of *that woman*. Money solved everything right up until the moment they found out I had given 99.5 percent of that money away to a charitable trust. After that, I was not just *that woman*, I was the woman who had denied David the life he *deserved*. I even had the gall to tell him he had to keep working, which meant when he was killed in the treatment plant explosion she sued me for causing his death.

For a while I was as angry with Piper Beauregard as I was with Mason McCoy, but eventually, I just felt sorry for her. And now I did the only thing I knew to do—I prayed for her to find peace.

Ah well, I had given Mr. Marshall and the bank's attorney good instructions on how to handle the ongoing demands they were making, and now it would be a waiting game to see if the Beauregards would respond the way I believe they will.

In my fridge, there is a couple of bottles of Lazy Magnolia pecan ales and some cracker barrel Colby jack cheese. I open a bottle of the beer and slice some cheese and scrounge up some club crackers. All of this I take through the flat with me to one of the tall skinny doors leading to the balcony. This is one of my favorite spaces; it has a black wrought-iron railing all around and is nearly overgrown with the ferns and bougainvillea draping down from the third floor balcony above. It is like being hidden in plain sight, and between the shading from the plants and the large blade ceiling fans, it stays fairly cool.

I sit down on one of the big wicker rocking chairs and put my now bare foot up on the railing. The nightlife is just starting down below on Bourbon Street, with the clubs opening their doors and shutters to let the sounds of the house bands float out. The restaurants are all full as the soon-to-be bar patrons start their nights with the other indulgence NOLA is famed for.

As I polish off the cheese and crackers and pop open my second beer, I spot the first ghost tour of the night. They are stopping at Jean Lafitte's, and I can see it is Kevin giving this tour. He's a fantastic guide and very good-looking. I believe that at least a hundred young women a year leave their hearts in the French Quarter.

As if he hears my thoughts, Kevin looks up to where I sit, and I stand up and part the vines and look down at him. He smiles up at me and salutes, to which I grin as big as I can and give him an "at ease, soldier". I love this part of living here in this crazy, eclectic, and neurotic town. We all watch out for each other and love each other no matter how incredibly different we all are. This is a town that I believe Jesus Christ would have a field day in. Not that there was just a lot of sin to heal because you can find that in every little town across this country. No, I think He would love it because there aren't a lot of stones being cast. There is a lot of caring for your neighbor, and charity runs deep here. I've had an easier time sharing my testimony of God's love and sacrifice and the pure, unadulterated message of Christ's forgiveness for all in this city than anywhere.

Just as the group are about to move on, Kevin surprises me and them both by coming over and climbing the railing up to my balcony and perching there to look back down at the group.

"Excuse me, ladies and gentlemen, just as you all just slacked your thirst in Pirate Lafitte's, I must also partake of sustenance." He looks over at me and winks. This is a skit we have played out once or twice. He pulls me into his embrace and makes a great showing of "drinking" from my neck. The ladies below gasp and secretly wish it was their nape Kevin was lavishing so much attention on.

"Geez, Kev, I've already showered today. Take it down a notch." I whisper as he finishes up by blowing a raspberry on the hollow of my neck. I can't help it, I giggle. Kevin has an infectious manner about him. He's really a kid at heart, but it's hidden behind cold blue eyes and long dark hair and sleeves of tattoos.

Now those cold blue eyes lock on mine, and he raises a jet-black eyebrow at me. "I could come back after the tour and finish this. I have until dawn, you know."

Since I'm still leaning over nearly backward, I reach up and put my hand on the strongest jaw line I've ever seen and sigh. Kevin would be so much fun.

"Sorry, Dracula, but I won't be responsible for the scads of broken hearts that would be left behind."

"Well, you can't blame a vamp for trying!" He spins me around, and I land in my chair, and he disappears over the railing. I hear many squeals and know that his daring has earned him copious tips.

I wander back inside the flat, wash my neck, and peel off my clothes except for my camisole. All the lights are off, but the glow from the street casts shadows in the room and across the king-sized bed against the interior brick wall. I stick my iPad into the docking station and start the playlist for my favorite blues artists. I lie back onto a pile of pillows and look at the play of lights and shadow across the ceiling and think about the totally unexpected detour of direction my life has taken the past few days. I was looking to bring peace to my soul, to be able to move forward from this stagnant and putrid place I have found myself in since that horrible day in Memphis. I firmly believe that forgiving Mason McCoy is all that stands between me and gaining control back over my life. I have already forgiven the others involved; they were easy to forgive, really, as they were fanatics caught up in what amounted to a fantasy, and they have shown great remorse. Besides, they have been served justice.

However, there is a long way between forgiveness and what I am currently feeling for Mason. I never, in a million years, would have guessed that I would have a nearly overwhelming attraction to him. It's stupid, really, how my body reacts to him. I mean, I've seen him on TV, and I've seen him in a couple of movies, and nothing made me think I would feel like this. Of course, seeing him that way doesn't prepare you for the raw emotions that are just under the surface, emotions that threaten to capture anyone in his path into their tide. Of course he's beautiful, but if beauty was all that mattered, Kevin was just as gorgeous and comes without the complications. No, it's the other that has drawn me in a way I can't seem to shake. But that doesn't mean I have forgiven him, and I now understand that it is going to take having the conversation and experiencing his reaction before I can really reach forgiveness.

Just as I am about to nod off, my phone rings, and I don't recognize the number. "Yes?" I answer.

"Hi." The now-familiar honey tones come through my phone, and I immediately get goose bumps.

"Hi yourself," I say, and I can hear the huskiness in my own voice. I hope he mistakes it for sleep and not what it truly is.

"Did I wake you?" Oh good, he does.

"I had just dozed off, but it's really early so no worries."

"Where are you?"

"In New Orleans."

"Asleep in the party city before 10 p.m.?"

"What can I say. I've had an exciting few days. I had to come here for some down time."

"I hear from my nephew that you started the day off with a little excitement. You've got the entire junior class of BSL High all atwitter about the new music director that rides a crotch rocket."

"Colton was a sweetheart. His mama has raised him right by the way. I was hoping to meet your brother, but he was busy."

"Colton is a great kid, thanks for saying so." I hear the genuine love and affection in his voice. He pauses for a few seconds during which I can hear him breath.

"Mason…"

"Dixie…" We both start to speak at the same time, but I urge him to go ahead and he repeats my name, and I love the way it sounds. "Dixie, I enjoy talking to you more than any other woman I know. I'm starting to think of you as a very close friend."

"Not everyone will understand that, and there could be fallout. Do you think it's wise, Mason?"

"Hell no! There's nothing wise about any of this, Dixie." His voice raises but then is immediately calm. "But I can't help it. I have to be able to talk to you and see you. There are just some complications that I will work through."

"Well, a wise person I once knew told me, 'Nothing worth having in life comes easily.'"

I hear the smile in his voice as he asks, "You think I'm worth having?"

"Right now, yes. I will let you know when and if I change my mind."

"I'll take it, Dixie Bryan. Now, I have a serious question to ask you."

I swallow hard past the lump that instantly appears in my throat. "Okay."

"Is that really Robert Johnson's 'Come in my Kitchen' playing in the background?" The question takes me completely off guard and launches us into a forty-five-minute discussion on the best all-time blues singers. In the end, we agree to disagree with me leaning toward Willie Dixon and he toward John Lee Hooker. It was spirited on both sides, and ultimately, I am incredibly impressed with his knowledge of the greats.

"I must go now, Miss Bryan. I've done my civic duty in keeping you up until the French Quarter minimum of 11 p.m." We both chuckle lightly at this. "Before I hang up though, I would like to know if we could have the jazz version of this discussion tomorrow night. I'll call you at nine?"

"I think that sounds like a great offer, Mr. McCoy. I look forward to it mightily." This time, we both laugh low and deep at how silly and formal our tone has become.

"Goodnight then."

"Night."

I lay my phone on the nightstand and am irrationally glad that I cannot see the ridiculous smile that I know is plastered on my face. Ugghhh.

Seventeen

The next morning I meet my friend Cindy and her beau, David, in a café very near the French Market. I fill them in on the progress I have made on the cottage and tell them about Michelle, Bob, and some of the other folks I have met in BSL.

"Giles misses you," Cindy tells me. "I didn't think the old coot had a heart in his chest, but he certainly has a soft spot for you."

"I'll stop by tonight and play a set with him. I miss him more than he could possibly miss me."

"So you decided to stay for a couple days?" Dale asks.

"Yes, I'm not heading back until Thursday night or Friday." As I say this, the waitress brings another round of *café au lait* and a plate of *beignets*. "I want to go see Randy and Paul while I'm here and drop in at the shelter."

After finishing our breakfast, we stroll through the markets, and I pick up some fresh produce, coffee, cheese, and freshly baked French bread. We part ways shortly afterward, and I walk back to the flat.

That evening, I arrive at the Funky Pelican early to help Cindy and her bartender, Marsha, get the bar ready before opening. While we are cutting up limes, lemons, and oranges, Marsha tells us hilarious stories she has heard from some of the more die-hard patrons. Being here feels like home, and these people are like my family.

An hour before the bands starts, the remaining members of our little group, Randy and Paul, come into the bar and sit at our table with us. We discuss the upcoming holidays, especially Halloween, which is a booming time in New Orleans. When I leave them to take the stage with the band, Randy is regaling the table with every detail he is putting into the Halloween party they are throwing.

Wednesday night I get back to my flat by 8 p.m. after eating a solitary dinner at my favorite restaurant, Mr. B's Bistro. Chef Michelle did her usual magic with some Bacon-wrapped shrimp over mascarpone cheese grits. Only the walk there and back to my flat would keep that indulgence from settling too hard on my hips. Not that I would care even if it did.

At eight-thirty, my phone rings and the caller-ID shows that it is Mason. I smile, thinking of the previous evening's phone call. I had called him before I left for the bar, and we had a short, but intense, discussion around best jazz musicians. I wasn't sure what genre we would be talking about tonight, but I was definitely looking forward to it, and I answer with a smile.

"Yo, M&M, ready to get your butt kicked again tonight?"

"Charming as always I see, Ms. Bryan." He laughs back at me.

"Who needs charm when you got a brain like mine?"

"*Touché*, madam." When he pauses, I hear lively music in the background.

"Where are you, Hollywood?"

"Actually, I'm walking down Rue Royal. I was hoping to talk you into having a drink with a friend."

It takes me several seconds to answer because my heart has dropped into my stomach. "Ah, sure. What'd'ya have in mind?"

"I like the Apple Barrel over on Frenchman's. Tell me where your place is, and I'll meet you, and we can walk over together."

I tell him to meet me at the corner of Royal and St. Phillip. The front of my building faces Royal, which will lead us straight down to Washington Square and Frenchman's street. Then I dash into the bedroom and pull off my sneakers, put on black motorcycle boots and change my long-sleeve tee for a dolman sleeved gray sweater and wrap a scarf around my neck. My hair is in a ponytail, so I improvise by putting it in a loose top knot. There. I don't look great, but it'll do.

When I spot him walking toward me, my heart skips a beat; he really is beautiful. His smile is perfect and white and pierces me straight through my center.

"Hey, M&M, this is an unexpected pleasure!" I say and give him a hug.

"I was afraid you might be angry for me dropping in on you or that you would be previously engaged."

I laugh because his language is so formal, after all, this is the man that called me a *turd* the night before when we were arguing over Miles Davis and John Coltrane.

"Of course I'm not mad. I'm delighted. It's not every night I get to listen to good music with a fellow aficionado."

We take off walking down the sidewalk, and we each point out some of our favorite shops and restaurants. Royal Street is only one block over from Bourbon, but it may as well be in a different time zone. I can hear some of the zydeco music, but the pace is relaxed here. We take our time and look into windows at some of the art and antiques on display, and by the time we get to the Apple Barrel, nearly forty-five minutes have passed.

There is a jazz trio playing, and they are incredibly good. We find a small table near the open window and settle in to order our drinks.

"Have you been here before?" Mason asks me.

"No, actually, I haven't. But I've heard about it. The acoustics are supposed to be phenomenal."

"Well, I am proud to open you to a new experience." He smiles, and then he takes his glass and holds it up for a toast. I lift mine in return, and he says, "I want to thank you, Dixie, for bringing fun back into my life." I am beyond surprised at these words but clink my glass against his.

"My pleasure, and thank you, as well. I've had more fun the past few weeks than I've had in years."

We both take drinks, but our eyes stay connected. Finally, I break the contact and turn back to look at the band. Soon we are commenting on the performance and how well they are doing. We have grown comfortable with each other, and our thoughts are very in synch with one another. When the band takes a break, Mason turns toward me and asks me an unexpected question.

"Just how tall are you, Dixie?"

"What?"

"Seriously, it's hard to tell when you are always wearing shoes that have a heel."

"I am five foot nine and three-quarters." Okay, I'm actually five foot ten but even after all these years, I am still a little sensitive about my height. "How tall are you, M&M?"

"One inch and one-quarter taller than you, which means when you wear heels, I get to imagine one of my favorite childhood fantasies."

"Oh boy, I can't wait to hear this one."

"I had the most intense crush on Wonder Woman you can imagine. Since then, I've always had a thing for tall brunettes."

"Which explains why you are dating a girl who looks more like Batgirl?"

A look crosses his face, and his eyebrows come down in the center, and I inwardly curse my penchant for saying every thought that crosses my brain out loud. He recovers quickly though.

"I wouldn't so much call it dating as I would babysitting."

I snort out loud at this, I can't help it.

"Besides," he says, "I had no idea Wonder Woman was available."

"Yeah, well, Superman left the toilet seat up one too many times. It was time to kick him to the curb."

This time it was him that laughed out loud, but the sound of it was lost as the music started up again. This time, as we turn to face the band again, he reaches over and takes my hand into his and squeezes.

Eighteen

It's nearly two in the morning before we leave the bar and head back toward my flat. We've both had a couple more drinks than we're used to so we lean slightly on each other as we stroll down the street. We compare notes on what we feel the best songs of the set were and, per usual, get passionate in our defenses. So passionate, in fact, that we don't notice the group of three men that have snuck up behind us until they break rank and surround us. Mason reaches over and grabs my arm to stop me.

"What do you want?" Mason asks in a low voice to the big blond that is standing in front of us. They look like college kids, but the look on their faces is anything but innocent.

"What you think, man? We want your money"—he looks over at me and growls—"and your woman." At this, the other two start laughing hysterically. It's clear that they are high on something.

I look around and see that the street is deserted. It's a Wednesday night during the off season.

"You can have my money, but you don't touch her." As he says this I start inching around until my back is up against Mason, and I am facing the other two punks.

"I don't recall giving you a choice, pretty boy." Lead punk says before he gives some signal to the other two.

They advance toward me, and I say, "Go, Mason." In one quick move, I rip a canister of tear gas out of a holder at my waist and spray it in an arc at their heads. They immediately drop to the ground, writhing in pain. I whip back around to douse the leader but stop in my tracks.

It takes a second for what I'm seeing to register. Mason is standing with his arm straight out in front of him, and the big blond creep is holding both his hands in the air and is making gulping sounds. I slowly take in the fact that at the end of Mason's hand is a pistol, and it is flush against blond boy's forehead. I am stunned because I never even felt Mason move. Blondie's lips are moving, but all I can hear is Mason speaking low and slow.

"I want you to go over and join your buddies on the ground there, then I want you to take your shoes and their shoes off and tie all the shoestrings together."

"Why, man? What're ya gonna do to us?"

"Nothing nearly as heinous as you was planning to do to us. Now, do it!"

I jerk as Mason yells, but it works to get Blond Boy moving. He does exactly as told, removing his shoes and those of his two buddies who are still writhing on the ground. Once they are all tied together, Mason takes them from him and turns to me.

"Let's go."

I nod at him, but just before we take off, I spray some of the tear gas on the back of Blondie's shirt. The overspray is enough to make him gasp and start crying in earnest. When I turn back, Mason is looking at me with a raised eyebrow.

"It's got UV dye in it and will make it easier for the cops to find them."

"Very nice." He remarks and then takes my hand, and we start running.

Once back at the flat, Mason calls the police while I grab two bottles of water out of the fridge. So as not to get involved, he tells them he saw some punks beating each other up and gave them the location.

"You can't miss them. They didn't have any shoes on." After he hangs up, we both laugh for a few seconds. And then I have a thought.

"Mason, where are you staying tonight?"

"I was going to drive back to Bay, but I may just go see if Royal Sonesta has a room. It's only a couple of blocks from here."

Before I think it out completely, I find myself saying, "Oh no, Mason, you can stay here."

Nineteen

While the words are still ringing in the air, we both go completely still. His gaze takes me captive for a few heartbeats, and the temperature in the room goes up a few degrees. The silly scarf I'm wearing feels too tight, but if I take it off I may as well hang a sign from my neck that says Wanton Woman. I watch him walk over to where I'm sitting, and I feel like everything is happening underwater. My hearing goes wonky and my breathing is suddenly labored. He sits on the couch next to me and reaches over and smoothes back a piece of hair that escaped the top knot.

Leaving his hand on the side of my neck, he whispers, "I was so scared they would hurt you, Dixie."

"I felt the same, Mason. I was so worried that I could only get two of them, but then I turn around and find out I was on a date with Dirty Harry!"

He smirks and says, "Oh please, you were the hero in this story. I got one guy and you wiped out two."

"Let's just say we are quite the crime-fighting duo—Wonder Woman and Batman." His eyes widen at this comparison. Then he leans forward and rests his forehead against mine, and we both shut our eyes and draw comfort from each other for a few minutes. Soon,

I feel his lips pressed against mine, and I sigh because it feels so right. The kiss deepens, and I feel my heartbeat quicken in response. In fact, it is so quiet that I swear I can hear his heartbeat as well. Our breathing starts to come quicker, and his hands are on either side of my head while mine are gripping his shoulders. Still the kiss goes on, and I feel myself leaning back against the couch. I feel Mason's hand run down my arm and come to rest on my waist. Every nerve ending in my body is sparking and building, and I know I need to stop this soon...okay, now.

I push Mason gently on the chest, and he seems startled, but he stops and sits back. We both work on getting our wits about us and our breathing under control.

"Can I tell you something, Dixie?"

"Of course, Mace." Considering you just had your tongue halfway down my throat, you can tell me anything I think.

"I think about kissing you all the time. I can't think of anything that I would prefer doing. I'd rather kiss you than eat, drink, or even breathe."

I don't answer. I can't; if I do, I will cry and then I might not stop. Instead, I get up and go into my bedroom and change into pajama pants and a tank top, grab a pair of cut-off sweats, and take them out to Mason.

He's pulled the sofa bed out and turns to look at me as I walk into the room.

"Here's something for you to sleep in." I say and toss him the pants. Then I go over to the wall closet and pull out a couple of blankets and pillows and help him make the bed up.

"I'll see you in the morning, Mason."

I slide the pocket door shut and lay down in my giant bed. It's very late, but I don't feel like I will be able to sleep. I run my fingers over my lips, which are still sensitive from the thorough kissing they were just put through.

Sometime later, I wake sitting straight up in the bed. The sound of screaming has woken me up, and I wonder where it's coming from about the same time I realize it's me.

"Dixie!" I hear my name just before the door to my room slides open, and Mason comes bursting through.

I blink at him as I get a grip on what's just happened. I haven't had a nightmare of this caliber in months. I close my eyes as I feel his arms go around me.

"Crap, Dixie, you scared me silly," he says this against my hair as he is holding me and stroking my arms. I feel myself calm considerably, and he lays me back down. Leaning on his elbow, he begins stroking my face and wiping the tears from my cheeks.

"It was just a dream, a bad dream. I haven't had this particular one in a long time." I look up at him, and his eyebrows are drawn together in concern. I reach up and rub the line that has formed there until it relaxes. When I look away from his face, I realize that he is wearing the shorts and nothing else. His chest is lightly covered with black hair. He is trim and toned with amazing muscle definition in his abs and arms. It works to take my mind off the dream, which I don't really remember anyway.

"It was probably brought on by the incident we had earlier," he says, and I realize his voice is still thick with sleep, and his eyes are drooping.

"Lay down, Mason. Go back to sleep. I'm going to be fine." I flip over on my side and reach behind me and take his hand and pull him over until he is lying right behind me. The heat from his chest against my back and his arm across my waist are both relaxing and distracting, but I draw a lot of strength and comfort from his presence and am soon sound asleep.

Twenty

It's nearly noon before I wake up. I smell coffee brewing and smile. I wander out into the living area and see that the door to the balcony is standing open. I fill a cup and sit down in the chair next to Mason.

He looks over at me and smiles. "Good morning, sunshine."

"Don't you mean afternoon?" I grin and sip my coffee. "Thanks for making this by the way. Despite the huge mess on top of my head saying otherwise, I feel human again."

He looks me over and chuckles. "Glad to be of help, ma'am."

We both sip our coffee for a bit, and then I look over at him. "Thank you, Mason. Thank you for being so great last night. You seem to know what to do in every situation."

His face gets hard for a second as he looks over at me, and then he sighs. "That's not really true though, is it? I pushed too far last night. I'm sorry, Dix, I really am."

"Well, I'm only sorry if what we did ends up hurting someone else." I give him a pointed look, and he winces. "But no use talking about this right now. I'm hungry. Let's go get some grub, and I'll give you a ride on my crotch rocket to your car." We both laugh at this.

Twenty One

I drive back to the beach cottage late Thursday afternoon. There's so much in my head that I am tempted to go straight up to bed. Instead, I pull on some shorts and running shoes and take off down Beach Boulevard. As I run west toward Waveland and the setting sun, I let my mind go over the mind-blowing direction my relationship with Mason has gone. I don't understand how I can feel so much attraction and, yes, affection even for this man; and yet, I can't be sure that I have fully forgiven him. I begin praying out loud.

"Father God, I can't even begin to thank you for the change in my feelings, for lifting my anger. I ask that you continue to work in me until the forgiveness I seek to give is true and real." Suddenly I feel a deep weight in my soul and the tears start flowing. "So I guess this is not going to be easygoing. Be with me. Help me to be wise and to not cause pain in your children. Most of all, I pray for your will to be done always. All these things I ask in your Son's perfect name, amen."

Friday night, Mason calls me earlier than our agreed time of 9 p.m. The discussion topic we said we would take on tonight is guitar greats. When his number pops up on my iPhone screen at 6:30 p.m., I am taken off guard.

"Hey, you, aren't you a little early?" I ask.

"Yes, sorry about that. I won't be able to call tonight. Something has come up." It's all I can do not to ask what, and he is clearly giving a pause for me to ask. I resist though. "But I actually have some good news. We have your bed done, and we found an old door we want to show you."

"That's awesome!"

"Well, just to let you know, it's an old warehouse door from the 1930s not an actual barn door."

"I'm sure it's perfect, but I will be able to tell within seconds."

"Good, so can you come see it tomorrow morning? If you can come by early to give the final approval, we can then come by and install the bed later in the day after the shop closes."

"Sure, sure. How does nine thirty work?"

"Perfect." He lets the pause hang for a second, and then he says, "I have to leave town tomorrow, Dix. There's an awards show I have to go to, and I have a couple of readings my agent is sending me to."

I feel a weird feeling in my chest as once again the reality of whom he is settles in. It's amazing how easily I have been able to ignore that side of his life. "Oh cool. Are you up for an award?"

"It's for my foundation for rescuing and rehabilitating animals."

"That's a noble cause, Mace. I'm happy for you that you're being recognized."

"I'm forcing the people that actually run it to go with me because they rarely get the praise they deserve. So it should be fun this time." I can hear the smile in his voice. After our lengthy phone calls, I have become intimately familiar with the tones in his voice that comes with the different emotions he is feeling.

"Are you excited about the scripts?" I ask because I suddenly find myself interested.

"One of them I'm very excited about because it will be a huge stretch for me. The other one I'm confident I can get if I want it, but"—and I can tell he is running his hand through his hair as he tries to think of the right words—"it's so in my wheelhouse that it won't be a challenge."

"And you're worried about being stereotyped?" I venture.

"Yes, I don't want to be seen as one-dimensional. Most of the scripts I get are of the bad boy, hot guy with a secret heart of gold."

I snort out loud. "You think you're hot, M&M?"

"Well, Miss Dixie, are you in the habit of making out with ugly guys?" I hear the playful tone and decide to go with it.

"Well, duh, Mason, haven't you heard? Nerds are all the rage these days. They get *all* the action."

I feel the change across the phone before he speaks again. "In that case, I will go get some braces and tape my glasses tomorrow if it means another make out session with you." Ahhhh! How does he manage to do that to me?

I clear my throat. "Didn't you say you had something to do tonight?"

"I have a few more minutes," he says, and I can hear the wriggling eyebrows.

"Well, then tell me about the script you are excited about."

He sighs at the change in subject, but I can tell he is pleased at my interest. "It's a book to movie adaptation. Normally I'd be skeptical about that because people are hardly ever satisfied with those." I can tell he is talking about himself in that group, and I have to agree. "But this is based on one of my favorite series, and the main character is the most complex and just one of the coolest guys ever invented."

"Sounds promising. Go on."

"He's an FBI agent, but he plays way outside the lines. He's from a very elusive and eclectic family in New Orleans, and he is definitely something that blurs the lines of human abilities—"

I have to interrupt him here. "Oh my goodness! Are you talking about Agent Guerin?" I can't help it. I squeal like a teenage girl. "I *love* those books, Mason. Oh, you have to get that part!"

I hear him chuckling. "Oh how I love your enthusiasm, Miss Bryan! And somehow I'm not surprised to find out you're a fan of the series."

"Awesome, awesome books, and I have such a crush on Aloysius. I am so excited for you. You just *have* to do this movie."

"Well then, I'll walk into the reading and tell the producer that it's decided, Miss Dixie Bryan of Bay St. Louis says I must get the part."

He and I both giggle at the silliness of this, and that is how we end the call with both of us smiling at shared good news between friends. It was the first time we had talked about his career, and I could feel how much he loved it.

It's not until I'm swinging in the porch bed and curled under the heavy quilt, later that night that I think of who will likely be with him in Los Angeles.

Twenty Two

The next morning, I get up early so I can spend some time stretching and going through some yoga poses out on the deck with Buddha. By 9:15 a.m., I am finishing some breakfast and ready to go see my new bed. I decide to drive the car so I can buy some of the wall hangings I had seen on my first visit to the store.

When I walk into the store, the bell rings, and a man looks up at me. I falter in my steps as I get a good look at him. He is so similar to Mason that it takes me completely off guard. His hair is a deep chestnut instead of black, and he is noticeably older, judging by the lines around his mouth, and the crow's feet that make him look like he smiles a lot. He is also broader and taller than Mason but so handsome that I am immediately in wonder that women don't stand at the window and gawk all day.

His face lights up, and he says, "So I can tell by the beautiful hair and how 'annoyingly' tall you are that you must be Dixie." He walks over and holds out his hand.

"That would be me, all right." I say back and smile broadly as we shake hands. "And there is no doubt that you are Johnny. Mason said you were his older brother, but he failed to mention that you were so much better looking than him."

"Well, the gene pool was a little shallow by the time he came along. Poor sucker is practically handicapped." The banter is easy and comfortable. I like this man immensely. We both chuckle, and then he says, "Are you ready to see your bed?" He motions me to a door in the back, and we enter a large workspace.

Mason is there, sanding the edges of a large wooden door. I immediately love the detail and the weathered wood of the door. I drag in a deep breath and tell them, "I really hope that door is meant for me because I will fight someone for it if not!"

Mason turns and breaks out in a huge grin. "I knew you would love it." I grin back at him and feel another chink fall. I ignore the warning siren that starts blaring in my head. Instead, I turn away from his baby-blue eyes and gleaming white teeth and see what must be my bed. Again, I am blown away by how well they have made my vision into reality.

The very low footboard is anchored on both sides by raw stumps that have been shaped and sanded and lacquered to a high shine. The headboard columns also contain stumps but much taller. The headboard itself is made from old wood siding that has been stripped and lacquered as well. Attached to the siding is an ornate wrought-iron fencing section. The iron is black weathered with rusted sections, and the points are topped with fleur-de-lis. It is absolutely perfect for the space. The stumps will make the bed look as if it is growing out of the floor.

I am speechless, and suddenly to my utmost embarrassment, I feel tears itching at the back of my eyes. I look around and both brothers are looking anxiously at me, and I know I should say something but to speak will mean crying.

Mason, better attuned to my feelings after all our conversations, seemed to understand. He looks at my wide eyes and walks over to take my hand and lead me over to the bed. There is an understated intimacy in the act, and I wonder briefly if Johnny has picked up on the connection between the two of us.

I run my hands over the smoothness of the stumps that contrasts nicely with the roughness of the reclaimed wood siding. The iron is a deeply historical addition. It looks like it was taken directly from a garden-district lawn. To set off the beautiful old *fleur-de-lis*, there is one branded into the center of the low footboard siding.

Having gained control of my emotions, I look from one to the other brother and say simply, "Thank you. It is perfect."

Johnny blushes a little and inclines his head. "You're welcome. If you're going to be home later this afternoon, Colton and I will bring it over and install it. Colton's recruited some friends to help us get it upstairs."

"That's perfect. I'll be home all afternoon. I have lots of yard work to do." I say this while feeling disappointment that Mason won't be with them. I do feel genuinely happy at the prospect of seeing Colton again.

As I leave, I pick up the two framed pieces I want for above the fireplace. Walking out, I hear my name and see Mason striding toward me.

"Hey," his voice is soft, and he puts his hand on my arm. I look behind him and see Johnny quickly turn his back to us. "Look, seeing you this morning made me realize just how much I'm going to miss you." He searches my eyes before continuing, "And I'm not sure how to deal with that."

I look from his eyes to his mouth and then down to his hand on my arm. I lay my hand over his and squeeze. I can't make myself address this right now because I still have a small part of me that ignites with anger at the idea that I might be responsible for his happiness of all things. But the part that is gleeful over him missing me dwarfs the anger, so I meet his eyes again and smile.

"I'm not going anywhere, Mason. I promise not to change my phone number and leave town while you're gone."

While I am talking, his eyes spark, and he says, "I believe that, Dixie, and it gives me a lot of comfort. But still…" He reaches up and runs a finger down my chin line along a scar that runs the entire length of my jaw. In response, my skin breaks out in goose bumps.

"Is it all right if I call you while I'm away?"

I put my hand over his and squeeze it before taking a step back.

"Of course," I reply and then I turn and get into my car without looking back. I am horrified by how much I am going to miss him.

Twenty Three

At home, I change into old cut-offs and a tee to work in the yard. I set my iPhone in the dock and choose an Elvis gospel album to play while I prune and cut the vegetation into submission. The work is gratifying but gives my mind the ability to concentrate on prayer. Being in nature, even in my own backyard, always puts me in a worshipful mood as I am awed by the beauty our Creator has blessed us with. Being grateful for anything is something I have had to work hard on the last couple of years, but I began with counting my blessings even if they seemed small things in the beginning. Small things add up to become huge things if you notice them.

So I thank God for the beautiful weather, the sweet smell of the honeysuckle that grows along the back fence, the soothing sound of the water feature, and the fact that I have my health again so that I can do all the work that needs to be done here. I thank Him for the changes he has brought about in my heart, the forgiveness that has started to bloom, and the fact that I feel some hope deep down that I will be happy again someday. I have tears streaming down my cheeks in recognition of all that he has given that I do not deserve in any way. I sit right where I am standing and close my eyes while I try to clear my head of thoughts. I have talked enough; it's time for me to listen.

Nearly an hour later, I stand up and stretch. My mind is clear, and I feel a renewed sense of purpose. I put all my cuttings in a compost bin and then feed the koi fish. I love the flash of scales in the sunlight and the way the water roils while they eagerly eat the small nuggets.

Deciding I most likely have time for a quick shower before Johnny and Colton show up with my bed, I make my way inside. Half an hour later, I am clean and dressed in comfy blue jeans and an old Dartmouth T-shirt with my hair pulled back in a ponytail. In the kitchen, I fill a giant Kerr Jar with sweet tea and take it with me to the piano and begin playing some blues.

I'm singing "Ain't No Sunshine," a classic from Buddy Guy, when the doorbell chimes just past five o'clock. I look up at the door and see Colton waving at me through the screen. He's adorable and looks so much like his daddy and uncle that I am amazed at how strong their genes must be. I am looking forward to meeting his mom, the principal, next week when I go in for a quick touch base about taking over the music program after Christmas break.

"Come in, please. I'm so happy to see you guys!" I greet them.

"Hi, Miss Bryan," Colton says and points to his two buddies. "These are my best friends, Luke and Danny." Coming in behind him are two boys that couldn't be more different. Luke is a stocky, broad-faced boy with dark, intense eyes and longish coal black hair while Danny is very tall and thin with white blond haircut in a high and tight military style. They both grin shyly at me in that way only a teen boy can look genuine doing.

"Hey, Luke, Danny," I say and smile back at them. "I really appreciate you helping Colton and his dad out."

"No problem," says Luke. "Mr. McCoy pays us to help him even though we probably owe him for all the meals Mrs. McCoy feeds us." This time the smile is big, and I can tell they really like Johnny's wife.

I look behind the boys and smile at Johnny and usher them all into the house and point up the stairs. "This is not going to be easy, I'm afraid."

Johnny looks up the stairs to the loft and then over at me. "We've had worse, trust me. At least your stairs are straight." He grimaces apparently from a remembered job that was difficult and then goes on, "Mason said you want the bed in the center of the loft?"

"That's right. With the footboard facing toward the front so the ocean will be what I see first thing in the morning and the last thing before I go to sleep." I catch his eye, and he crinkles them up in a smile.

"I can relate, Miss Bryan," is all he says, and then he is herding the boys out to the truck, and they come back, carrying various pieces of the bed, which they reassemble in the loft.

Nearly an hour later, I have a place to sleep inside my house. I know I will miss sleeping on my porch, but I am excited about the prospect of waking up to a view of the morning sun glistening on the bay waters.

As they are gathering their tools and preparing to leave, Colton walks over to my piano and asks me a surprising question, "Do you know Thelonius Monk's music?"

"I do as a matter of fact. He's the greatest jazz pianist of all time. I'm a little surprised that you do, Colton. I don't know any other kids your age that listen to Monk or jazz for that matter."

He blushes slightly under my gaze. It makes him even cuter, and I bet the girls at Bay High School live for that blush. "Uncle Mason got me started listening to jazz and blues a few years ago."

"That's wonderful, Colton. You're gonna make for a very interesting student, then. Do you play an instrument?"

"I've been taking piano lessons since I was seven years old, but I'm not very good."

When he says this, Johnny stops and looks over at us and frowns. "Now, Colton, that's not true." He looks at me and says, "He is very talented, Miss Bryan. Don't let him kid you."

I smile at Johnny because his obvious pride in his son is palpable, and then I raise my eyebrow at Colton. "Since I am the teacher, I will quite literally be the judge of that!"

"Okay, okay," he said while holding his hands up in front of him.

We all walk toward the door, and I thank them again for bringing the bed over. Johnny told me that he thought they would be ready to install the warehouse door and the window-seat drawers later the following week. I was excited to hear this and just as I was thinking what a wonderful evening I'd had, Johnny says, "By the way, my wife says she is really looking forward to you coming by the school next week. She says you have a fascinating academic background. Sandra really gets excited about that kind of thing." Then he rolls his eyes and shakes his head.

I make myself smile and chuckle with him and the boys, and then I wave good-bye as they walk down the path to their pickup.

So Sandra King, sister-in-law to Mason McCoy, says I have an interesting background. My stomach flops as I wonder just how much of my background she may have discovered. I suddenly have a very interesting meeting coming up.

Twenty Four

S unday morning, I wake up and take some time getting ready for church. I use the big round brush to get to a close proximity of the soft curls Jean-Luc had created. Today will be my first time singing in the choir, and I want to look my best. I'm nervous, and I pray the whole way there that I will not let Nell down.

After Sunday school in which we studied 1 Corinthians 13, one of my very favorite passages, I slide into the choir section. Nell grins at me and leans over and asks, "You ready for this, Nola?" Nola has become her nickname for me since finding out that is where I was living prior to moving to BSL.

"You bet I am, Nell." I say just as the piano starts up with what will be a full six-minute rendition of "Jesus Loves Me." I have a short solo right in the middle, and it goes off without a hitch. I soar a little and growl a little, and it feels so good that I am crying by the end of the song, so thankful that God has given me this ability and an outlet to worship Him.

Twenty Five

Tuesday morning dawns with abundant sunshine and crisp temperatures in the 60s. I am both nervous and excited to go speak with Sandra at the high school. The prospect of teaching is giving me more pleasure than I imagined, and I am very impatient for the new semester to start.

However, I am approaching the meeting with the principal with some trepidation. If she is aware of my full background, then I'm sure she will have many questions for me that I am not sure I'm ready to answer just yet.

I take extra care with my hair and put on a little makeup as though I am trying to prove my worth through my looks. Ridiculous, but that is the way women operate around each other, isn't it?

At 10 a.m. precisely, I enter the office at Bay High School. Sandra's assistant, Beth, greets me with a big grin.

"So you're Miss Bryan!" she enthuses. "We've heard so much about you already." Before I can react to that, she goes on, "Everyone here is so excited to get some young blood in the Glee Club."

"Glee Club?" I ask because I wasn't aware that the school had one.

"Well, it's technically choir, but since that TV show came out, we've all been calling it that." She looks slightly embarrassed, but when I grin at her, she relaxes.

"I'm a fan of that show too." I say and wink at her just as Sandra comes out of her office.

She is a very handsome woman. She has short curly hair, cut in a very stylish bob, and it is very blonde. She has a light scattering of freckles that give her a youthful appearance. She has smile lines and, although Colton looks so much like his dad, I immediately see that his lips and the color of his eyes come directly from his momma.

She walks over with her hand out, and I shake it. "Hello, Dixie. It's so good to finally meet you!"

"The feeling is mutual. Although I feel as though I already know you from all the phone conversations."

"Come with me to my office, and we can chat before I take you to see where your classroom will be."

We enter a large, organized space. I take a seat across her desk and see several pictures of her family on the bookshelves behind her. One of those pictures is of Mason and Hanna. I swallow the lump that has suddenly formed in my throat.

Sandra has noticed the direction of my gaze and says, "My family, as motley as they are." And she grins warmly. Then she turns to look at me, and I see the warmth drop a degree or two before she continues. "I understand you have met most of my family already?"

"Yes, and they are wonderful. I stumbled across your husband's store, and they've been building some furniture for me."

"Thanks for that. Johnny loves projects, and he has been completely immersed in your job."

"Well, I am the one benefitting. I think the work is pure genius."

"It's the one passion he and his brother share. I've been pleased to see them working together so much." Then she kicks her head to the side while looking at me. "Sort of strange that I have you to thank for that."

Oh crap. Well that answers my question of what she found from my background check; it must have been thorough. My palms get sweaty immediately as I realize I am going to be talking about *the incident* for the first time since it happened. For a time, we just sit and look at each other.

"So. I guess you have some questions for me?" I say with a raised eyebrow.

"I'm not sure, honestly," she says this on an exhale of breath and leans back in her chair. She looks over at her computer, back at me, and then crosses and uncrosses her legs. She looks nervous, but there is an undercurrent of anger there as well, and that is what my emotions respond to, and I feel myself working up a good *mad*.

"I can't fathom what your angle here could be, Mrs. Beauregard," she says, and I can't help it, I flinch when she uses my married name. "I was devastated over what happened to you as was my family"—she looks directly at me now—"but no one as much as Mason." Now she sits up in her chair and leans forward. "If you are here to punish him in some way, you need to know that he has, and still is, suffering over that event. In fact, my husband and I thought for a while that he might, well, harm himself." As she finishes this statement, I can't help it. I am overcome with fury.

"Harm himself?" I shout and then, from much practice, immediately get control. "Harm *himself*?" I repeat with a growl. I stand up and yank my blouse out of my pants and hold it up so she can see the twisted scar tissue that covers my stomach and left rib cage. Even after all this time, it is ugly and knotted and pink. She jerks her head, and I see tears in her eyes.

"I'm so sorry," she says. It makes me madder.

I hiss out the words, "Do you have *any* idea what it feels like to have a bomb go off *in your arms*? Any idea of the blinding, deafening, searing pain of shrapnel flying through your skin, and even worse, the knowledge that what is protecting your organs and keeping you alive is the tough walls of the expanded uterus carrying your first and *only* child's body?"

I stand, nearly over her now, and my breath is coming in gulps. Her face has lost all its color, and the tears are now spilling over her lashes.

I suddenly fall back into the chair as the fury leaves as quickly as it came on. "You will have to excuse me if I'm not as concerned about Mason as you are, Sandra."

"Oh, Rexanna, please don't. Don't apologize. It should be me apologizing to you. I can't fathom the horror of what you went through."

I look at her, and I can see that she is being genuine. I know that as a mother, she can in some way understand.

"Please, don't use that name. I haven't been Rexanna Beauregard since I buried my husband and my child."

We sit in silence for what feels like hours until she asks me *the* question.

"Why are you here, Dixie?"

I sit and think about this for about thirty seconds. I want to test it out and make sure that it is still the truth before I commit to it out loud.

"I am here to forgive Mason."

I can tell she is taken off guard by this as am I to be honest. Still. I can only trust God.

"Are you serious? You want to forgive him?"

"No, I don't want to do anything of the sort, but I have to. The anger and bitterness has become a handicap to me. I can't move forward with my life, my happiness, and most importantly, my relationship with God until I do."

She stares at me for seconds, and then she begins crying more earnestly. And like a dang traitor, my eyes begin leaking as well.

"I don't believe it, Dixie. I have prayed and prayed for this to happen. I simply prayed for you to be able to forgive and move forward. I never expected to actually know that you had, never expected to get to know you, and see it happen."

"Well, don't get ahead of yourself. I haven't reached the point that I can forgive him just yet."

At this she looks confused. "But Johnny said that you and Mason have been seeing each other and that Mason can't talk of anything else."

"He doesn't know who I am, Sandra. I haven't talked to him about what happened because I'm not ready." I stand up and start pacing around her office. I am running my hands through my hair and destroying all the work I put into that morning.

"I'm getting to know him, and I like him. Amazingly enough, we are fast becoming best friends." At this truth, I shake my head at the unlikeliness behind the words. "But as you just saw, I still carry a lot of resentment and anger, and I don't know if I can truly let it go." I turn and look at her to see if she understands. To my relief, she nods.

"You lost so much. I would be amazed if you could. Except that you obviously believe in God and the power He has in our lives." She gets up and walks around to me and puts a hand on my arm and looks right into my eyes, which is something I have a hard time with still. "He can bring the healing, and I believe He has a miracle in store. He does His best works in the middle of tragedy."

I look back at her for a long time, and finally I nod, more to myself than to her, but I feel a spark of hope ignite. For the first time since the plant my husband ran exploded, I have been completely honest with someone, and it feels good.

"Well, Ms. Bryan, let's go have a look at your classroom."

Twenty Six

Two hours later, I feel very familiar with the layout of Bay High. I met my predecessor, and he is quite happy to hand over the reins. I have seen where I'm gonna spend forty-to-fifty hours per week for the duration of this next chapter of my life. I have taken inventory and know what instruments I plan to purchase and bring back with me. Also, Sandra and I have agreed to change the name of the choir to Glee Club in order to take advantage of the popularity of the television show. We discussed the idea of having auditions for the club, and I plan to hang an Open Audition Call sign-up sheet and begin taking appointments between now and the end of the semester. I hope to have the club filled by then so we can start the second half practicing for a gala that Sandra told me they have at the end of the year. I feel like I will have my hands full between the music appreciation class and the Glee Club, but I can't wait for it to start!

As we walk back into her office, Sandra picks up her purse and says, "Are you free for lunch?"

I'm more than a little surprised, but I say, "Yes, of course, boss." She busts out laughing.

"Puhleeeze, Dixie, my husband is the only one that calls me that." We both chuckle at the understated truth behind that statement. She goes on, "And I would really like it if you'd call me Sandy."

"Okay, Sandy. That fits you really well."

Ten minutes later, we are sitting at the lunch counter of the local butcher-and-deli shop. We decide to split one of their huge club sandwiches and sip on ice cold sweet tea while we wait for the meat to be sliced.

She looks over at me and smiles a sweet smile, and suddenly, the reality of the moment hits. I am having lunch with a woman who knows the truth about me. Not only knows who I am, but the *complete* truth about who I am. And just like that, the back of my eyes start to itch, and I feel tears threatening.

"You wanna talk to me about what's going on with you and Mason?" she asks as if she could see straight into my brain. I take a deep breath and sit back in my chair. Just when I can't hold it anymore, I blow it back out and look down at my hands.

"I don't even know where to start, Sandy. I mean, I don't even understand myself. How does a person go from hating another human being with a white-hot passion even to the extent that you become violently ill when you see an image of that person to…to this?"

"What exactly *is* this? Tell me how you feel now," she asks, and she has such a genuine emotion on her face that I decide to jump in with both feet.

"I am insanely attracted to him as are thousands upon thousands of young women and men for that matter. But I can't explain what I feel by just his looks.

That is such a small part of his appeal. He has this amazing ability to make you feel as though you are the most important person in the world when he's with you. His mind is amazing, and he has exquisite taste. He feels things so intensely, and I love how much he loves his family and his heritage. I don't know, Sandy, he just cares so deeply." I stop here because I realize I'm not getting it right somehow. "You know, it comes down to the fact that had I met Mason earlier in life, say in college, I honestly believe that we would have been the best of friends."

Sandy reaches across the table and squeezes my hand. The look on her face is something close to relief. I think she has been halfway wondering if I was faking my plan to forgive Mason.

"So, Dixie, tell me what you plan to do."

"I'm going to tell him. I have to tell him, but I need more time. I can imagine it seems selfish, but I have to make sure the forgiveness is real first." I look at her and will her to understand. To my vast relief, I can see that she does. However, there is a problem, and we both know it.

I say, "I won't be upset though if you need to tell the truth. I can't possibly expect you to keep secrets from your family."

She sits back and drapes an arm across the chair. She studies me for a minute and her cool green eyes seem to be looking deep into my head.

"Dixie, I feel like you have probably been more honest with me today than you have been with anyone in a long time." I nod my affirmation to her and she goes on, "So I am going to return the favor. Johnny says that Mason is very taken with you. He says, in fact, that he has never seen him quite so full of hope."

I look sharply up at her when she says this.

"Yes, I said hope. Let me explain. Mason had his heart shattered by his first Hollywood girlfriend. She was his co-star in his second movie. It was a smallish part in a big production, but he stole the show, and Lauren snapped him up. She was older and a much bigger star, but Mason is just so adorable and *photographable*. He got her into the tabloids, and they became a darling couple. The problem was that Mason was in love with the character she played, and she wasn't in love with him at all. It shouldn't have been that big of deal, but it was his first public relationship, and he couldn't separate the reality from what was fabricated. This went on for nearly two years, but eventually, she was photographed in another country with another man, just when Mason was working up a plan to ask her to marry him. He found out by seeing photos on *Access Hollywood*." She takes a deep breath and looks around us. Satisfied that no one was paying attention to us, she continues, "On its own, that probably wouldn't have caused his breakdown, but it was about that time that Johnny and Mason's sister died, and then shortly after that the waste plant exploded."

I flinch as the words are spoken aloud. She reaches out and squeezes my hand again but continues on, "And then he just got so angry. He put all that grief and anger into the contamination. He became obsessed with the news and began blogging and tweeting nonstop. He would find names and post them and encourage his followers to send e-mails and letters and to start boycotts and petitions. And then of course, he was getting all kinds of publicity because he was from here. The tabloid shows loved that he was a local and deemed him an expert. His manager and publicist encouraged him through it all." She looks up at the ceiling and shakes her head. "Johnny and Bob tried so hard to talk him down, after all we were down here and saw first hand what the divisiveness was doing to the community, and most importantly, we saw what the clean-up companies were doing, and how hard they were working." Now she stops and closes her eyes before saying, "Then the news came out about your husband. What his part in the explosion was and that his widow stood to receive millions in a settlement and Mason just lost it. His blog and tweets about you were horrible." She is crying now, and I feel sick remembering.

We both know the next chapter of the story: a group of radical environmentalist had latched onto Mason's blogs and was able to find out where David's funeral was going to be held. They waited until I was walking to the hearse and sent a young woman to hand me a beautiful white teddy bear. She simply said, "For your baby" and walked off. Five seconds later, the bear exploded, ripping through my abdomen, killing the little girl I had been carrying for seven months and very nearly killing me. The picture they showed on all the news channels was of my black-clad, bloody and torn body lying on the sidewalk in front of the two-hundred-year-old church, still wearing my black veil, the sun glinting off my diamond wedding ring.

I quietly get up from the table and go to the ladies room where I vomit up my lunch.

Sandy is standing outside the door with my purse when I exit. We walk in silence to her SUV.

"He went a little crazy when he found out what happened to you, Rexanna. Sorry, I mean Dixie. And he probably deserved it. He took down his blog and cancelled all his appearances. He carried around that awful newspaper photo for months, and he vowed to find you. He said he wanted to apologize and try to do something, anything to help, but I think he really wanted to give you the opportunity to hate him in person. But you did a great job of disappearing."

This was true. In the hospital, I was under guard by the FBI, and then I left the country. A dear friend gave me refuge at his compound in Costa Rica, and no one could get near me.

"I went where no one could find me. I was in a place mentally that I didn't want anyone else to know, and I wasn't sure I was coming back. If you follow."

"I believe I do. It's not so different from the emotions I watched Mason go through. He also secluded himself by immersing himself into that show that takes him to a far away island."

By now, we are pulling into the school parking lot. I pull on the door handle, and she stops me by putting a hand on my arm.

"Dixie, listen. I don't know what he will do when he finds out, but I imagine it will be a huge shock, and he may overreact." She looks past me to the huge live oak tree in the courtyard and then looks back directly at me. "I won't say anything about this unless I am directly asked. I trust you, my friend. I trust you to do the right thing in the right way. You've earned the right to do what you want to do with this. God knows you paid an unfathomable price. So it's between you and Mason now."

We both exit the car, and as I head toward mine, I turn and ask my last question.

"What about Hanna?"

Sandy looks confused for a second then starts laughing. "Oh my goodness, I forgot all about that. Their relationship is all for show, Dixie. The studio thought it would be good for the ratings if the world thinks the bad boy of the island and the sweet good girl are an item off screen. He finds it exhausting, but it has worked." She walks into the building still chuckling, but I am not as comforted as I should be. After all, I remember a conversation starting with the words *sweetheart*.

That night, Mason calls my cell, but I don't answer. I am not ready to talk to him because he would sense something was wrong. I don't answer the next night or the night after that either. Mason isn't the only one I avoid. I don't leave the house or talk to anyone for three whole days. The anger has returned not as strong, but its there. I am grieving again still, but as unlikely as it sounds, I am grieving for Mason as well as myself. I remember the raw pain on his face the night we kissed in my kitchen, and it makes me sad for the innocence he lost along with me. I am also grieving in advance for the loss of him in my life when I tell him the truth. Sandy made me feel certain that is what will happen. Just because I will forgive him doesn't mean he will.

Twenty Seven

Finally, on Thursday, I called him.

"Dixie! Where've you been?" he said by way of greeting.

"I've been…busy. And I needed some time to myself to sort some things out." That was the truth, but I knew he would take it another way.

After a slight hesitation, he said, "So you too, huh?" Then he chuckled lightly.

"What do you mean?" I ask.

"Just that there seems to be a lot of that going around. I've been doing lots of thinking the past week myself. The difference is that I wanted to talk it out with a great friend of mine." I can hear the hurt behind the teasing.

"I'm sorry, Mace. Really, I am. But I'm a little mixed up about some things, and the way I deal with it is by holing up and doing demolition and construction." At this he laughs and asks what I have been constructing. I tell him about all the work I'm doing in the backyard. When we reach a minute of silence, I can feel a change of mood from his end of the phone. When he speaks, his voice tones are lower and calmer.

"Dixie, do you miss me?"

"Of course I do, Mason."

"Why?"

"Because no one else will debate me on the worst pop stars of the 80s the way you do."

"Anything else?"

"I miss you being here in my house, cooking for me, and being an accomplice in trying new wines. I miss your laugh too." I can't bear to go on, so I say, "Your turn now. Do you miss me?"

He breathes into the phone for a couple of beats, and when he answers, his voice has taken on the tone that does funny things to my stomach.

"In more ways than you can imagine, darling."

I can't help myself, I say, "Why don't you tell me then." I have to swallow past the lump that has formed in my throat.

"I miss hearing the smile in your voice when you say my name. I miss making you laugh, and I miss how dang mean you can be when ridiculing my musical taste."

At this I laugh and say, "I'm not mean! You are just stunningly ill-informed on certain genres."

"See that? I miss that. I also miss cooking in your awesome kitchen and drinking your experimental wine choices"—he sighs and goes on—"I really miss watching you do that thing you do with your lips after you've taken a sip, and I miss the way your eyes turn a deeper green after you've had a second glass."

My heart is thumping in my chest, and my breathing is a little shallow, and still, he goes on.

"I totally miss that amazing hair that is so thick my hands could disappear into it, and I really, really, really miss how it felt to kiss those amazing soft lips."

"Mason,"

"No, Dix, you had your chance. Still my turn. Let's see I mostly miss how when I'm with you or talking to you. I don't want to be anywhere else on earth. You settle me, and it is so surprising."

I am crying now. Something has opened in my chest, and it is on fire, spreading warmth throughout my body.

"Dixie?" I hear the concern in his voice.

"Oh Mace."

"Are you crying, Dixie?"

"No, I mean, yes. I mean…"

"Hey, hey, it's okay. I know I just dumped a ton on you. We need to talk about this more, but it can wait."

"Okay, that's good. We can do that."

"I'm going to be there Friday. Will you go out with me that night?"

"Umm, sure, where do you want to go?"

"Dancing," he says, and I about fall out of my seat. "There's a club in the casino on the north side of town. I have something to celebrate, and I feel like dancing. Will you go? Please? Pretty please with sugar on top?" Oh boy, how do you resist that?

"Well, since you said the magic word…"

I can hear him grinning as he says good-bye and ends the call.

Twenty Eight

I t's 7:30 p.m. when my doorbell rings Friday night. Mason is standing on the front porch in a pair of designer dark denim jeans, fitted black button up, and black boots. He looks like the beginning of a dirty dream, and I blush just looking at him. He purses his lips and cocks his eyebrow as he looks me over.

"You'll do." He smirks.

"Whatever, M&M," I say because I know that I look pretty darn good. I took my time with a curling iron and created a mass of long curls. I even broke out the eye makeup to make my eyes look dark and smoky. Even I can appreciate the difference it made.

In light of the dancing we would be doing, I am wearing a pair of well broke-in Levi's 501s and a black halter top that has a loose empire waist. I didn't want anything restricting my movements.

Mason looks down at the comfy black kid-leather boots I'm wearing and murmurs appreciatively. "At least you aren't wearing heels." Then he looks back up at me and winks, setting off thousands of butterflies in my belly.

At the casino, we stop in the steakhouse for a light meal and a couple of cocktails. I order a Jameson Gold, and he raises his eyebrows.

"I remember that's what you were drinking the night I saw you with Bob and Michelle."

"Yep," I answer. "Good whiskey is a lot like good wine in that you should be able to appreciate the individual ingredients that combine to create such complex flavors." I smile at him over my glass as I sip the mellow liquor. When I lower the glass, his gaze stays on my lips. I hope he mistakes the flush creeping up my chest to be from the potency of the whiskey.

I'm saved when the pretty young waitress stops by our table for the umpteenth time to ask Mason if there's anything else he needs. I think it's funny and more than a little sweet, and I tell him so.

"You don't find it annoying?"

"Of course not, Mace. I mean it comes with the territory, doesn't it?" When he nods, I go on. "Its young women like her that makes you the star you are. The power you have from that comes with a lot of weight and obligations but also a lot of perks. I personally think one of the perks is the difference you can make in a life. If you take a couple seconds and say something encouraging to her, it could make a lasting difference in ways you wouldn't expect."

Mason curls his lips inward and gazes at me for a few seconds and then picks up his glass in a salute. "You are going to be an amazing teacher, Dixie Bryan."

I raise mine in return and say, "That reminds me. You said you had something to celebrate?"

"Yes, yes, I do. Actually *we* have something to celebrate."

This confuses me, and I cock my head to the side and squint my eyes. "We?"

"Absolutely, this is your victory as much as mine. I got the part, Dixie! I am going to be playing Special Agent Guerin."

I start clapping and squealing like a little girl. I can't help it. I wanted this so much for him and had prayed that it would happen, but I certainly didn't expect it to happen so quickly!

"Oh my gosh, Mason, this is fantastic news! I knew you could do it!"

He's grinning so big, and his excitement is oozing out of his pores. He reaches across the table and takes my hand, and he gets a little more serious.

"Dixie, I owe much of this to you."

"Oh no, Mace"

"Yes, yes, I do. Your advice to get into character, to go in with the white blond hair, and the clothing. Well, it did it for me. You were so right when you said I needed to take away the need for them to have to imagine what I would look like in costume. The author was there, and he was blown away by how closely I fit his idea of what Aloysius would look like."

"I was just afraid they would be stuck on how dark you are, and the books describe him as being so pale. But your eyes are exactly the shade I imagine when I read those books. The eyes are the most important thing to match. Everything else can be changed with makeup and hair dye." Then I look up at him quickly and say, "Wait a minute, how did you fake the white-blond hair?"

"I was in Hollywood, baby. I went to hair and makeup at the studio, and they put a great wig on me." We both laugh at that.

"Ahhh, Mason, I am now over anxious for you to do this movie! I will be the first person to buy a ticket!"

"You won't be buying a ticket. You'll be at the premier as my guest. In fact, I may have to make you a consultant since you seem to be so intimately familiar with Guerin." He wriggles his eyebrows, and I can't help but laugh.

I giggle but then sober up as I admit, "I am! Oh, Mason, you have no idea how big of a crush I have on him. I read all their books, one right after another a couple of years ago, then I go back and read one every month or so."

"You sound like me. I have a set of hardbacks on my bookshelf, but I read paperback versions, and they are about to fall apart."

We grin across the table at each other and finish off our drinks. As Mason pays the check, I ask him the burning question.

"So, Mason, are you a good dancer?"

"I've been told I'm pretty good."

"Really? Do you slow dance, line dance, or do you get jiggy?"

"I don't line dance," he says and twists his lips up to the side. "How about you, Dixie, do you think you can dance?" I laugh at his pun and then put on my serious face.

"I don't just think I can dance, I know I can dance. I've been dancing since I could stand up." This is the truth. My parents weren't like other parents. Both were intensely intelligent, but both had Asperger's Syndrome, so their social maturity was stunted. My youngest memories were of dancing nonstop around the living room with them while the record player blared in the background. Even after I had to go live with my grandparents, I would still shut myself away in my room and dance with my cassette-player headphones on. Dancing and music was my escape.

"I do have to warn you, Mason. The music completely takes me over when I dance. I blank out my mind and just move." I'm serious, and he looks a little surprised at what I said. "Really, I don't want you to be too shocked by what I do in there."

Now he looks a little uncomfortable, and I have to laugh. He looks like he's imagining a sordid past.

"Wait, before you go and get too scandalized, I'm not talking about dancing on a pole or anything!"

"All right, Ms. Bryan, you have me intrigued. Let's go see what you got."

Twenty Nine

When we walk into the dance club, the floor was almost full, but we easily slip into the crowd. The speakers are pumping out "Harder to Breathe" by Maroon 5, and I immediately feel my bones liquefy and my muscles take over. I close my eyes and feel the percussion thump in my chest, setting the tone for my movements. Soon I forget that there are other people present, and it's as if I'm a fifteen-year-old at college dancing in my dorm with my headphones on all over again. The next song is "Let It Rock" by Kevin Rudolf, and I begin to feel my hair sticking to my neck. I am so at ease moving on the dance floor though that I don't slow down one bit. This goes on through two more songs and then "Summer Love" by Justin Timberlake starts playing. The beat is much slower but still fairly funky. I turn around and Mason is right there, close enough that our chests touch, and I can smell the sweetness of his breath. The music has me snaking my body against his, and he responds in kind. Our eyes never leave one another's, and I run my hands up his arms and cup his face. I have never wanted to kiss anyone this much in my whole life, but I hold back. He buries his hands in my hair and pulls my face toward his. Our noses are touching, and still we don't kiss, just keep moving gently to the music and breathing in each other's breath. It's hypnotic, and the rest of the nightclub fades into oblivion. The phrase *heiros gamos* flashes in my mind, as I definitely am feeling like the ying to his yang. I faintly register the change of music to "Scandalous" by Prince, and it think it very appropriate because scandalous is how I am feeling.

My eyes close, and I turn my head up a little more to make it easier for him to kiss me, and just then, I hear a curse word come out of his mouth and see a flash from behind my eyelids. They spring open in time to see Mason grab a guy by the back of his shirt. The man is holding an expensive camera, and I follow as Mason marches him off the dance floor.

"What the heck, man?" he shouts.

"Dude, you're in a public place. Fair game." The man says as he tries to grab the camera back from Mason, who is flipping through the frames and erasing pictures. As he does this, I am thinking how the heck did he get so many pictures of us without me noticing?

Mason hands the camera back to the guy, who is complaining loudly by now. Luckily, two burly bouncers come over and take him away. I look at Mason, who is pinching the bridge of his nose and looking at the floor. I hate that our privacy was invaded, but I don't understand why he is so upset. And then it hits me like a ton of bricks.

"Mason, are you worried that Hanna will see a picture of us together?" I know what Sandy told me, but I still feel like there may be some kernel of truth to their relationship.

He looks incredibly pained when he answers me, "Yes. I don't want it to end this way."

I put my hands into my back pockets and nod my head. How could I have ignored this for so long? Here I've been singing my little *Song of Solomon*, and in truth I'm just a Jezebel. Is it really possible that I had gotten things so wrong?

"Well, that's good, Mason. I wouldn't want to be that person, either, so I guess we are on the same page there." I turn and walk over to the bar, where I ask if they can call me a cab, then go back to where Mason is still standing, staring after me.

"Congratulations on your movie, Mason. I really mean that. And I really mean it when I say I want to be your friend. But I can't keep doing this. I won't be that woman. So please don't call me for a few days. I think I need to detox you out of my system."

Then I walk past him toward the door. At the last second, he grabs my arm and stops me. I turn my head, and our eyes slam into each other, and it's like neither of us has the heart to look away. Finally, I feel tears threatening, and I pull my arm loose.

"Good night, Mason."

Thirty

I wake up to stormy skies Saturday morning. I put on some Nina Simone and lay back down and watch the gray seas rolling in. I reach over and pick up my mobile phone and see that I have seven missed calls. Six are from Mason, and one is from Michelle.

Michelle knew that I was going out with Mason the night before, and I know she wants the details, but I don't have the heart to discuss it with her. I'm just not ready to dissect what happened.

I must have drifted back to sleep because I am startled awake by knocking on the front door sometime later. I spring up from bed and grab my robe before heading down the stairs. I stop just shy of the bottom step when I see Johnny McCoy and his son, Colton, standing on the front porch. Crap! I forgot they were coming to install the door in the hallway today.

I reach up and try futilely to smooth down my hair a little before answering the door.

"Hello, I am so sorry for making you wait. I overslept, obviously, which is something I never do!"

Johnny takes in my robe and mussed hair, and bless his heart, he peers past me and looks up the stairs as if he expect there to be a man slinking around up there.

I clear my throat and say, "Come on in, you two. I'll put on the coffee and get out of your way."

Colton is grinning as he comes in with his tool belt slung around his hips. I'm sure he's committing this episode to memory for when he gets in trouble in my class. His dad has regained his composure enough to speak briefly and tell me what their plans are. Turns out he plans to build the window seats while he is here, as well. I'm thrilled with this while at the same time, I feel unsettled to be around two men that remind me so much of Mason.

While they are working downstairs, I shower in the upstairs bathroom. I look at myself in the mirror first and see that my eyes are puffy from crying so much last night. I also didn't take off my makeup, so I have mascara halfway down my face. Uggghhhh! No wonder Johnny acted like I was a crazy person. I look the part.

Twenty minutes later, I am showered and my teeth are brushed, and I can smell the wonderful smell of Pumpkin Spice coffee brewing down below. I pull on some yoga pants and a New Orleans Saints tee and head downstairs.

I'm pouring a big steaming mug of coffee when a voice behind me says, "Dixie."

I nearly drop my mug, splashing hot liquid on my hand. "Dang it!" I shout while flipping open the cold tap at the sink and sticking my hand under the water. I glare at Mason to let him know how upset I am with him.

"I'm sorry! I shouldn't have snuck up on you like that," he says.

"No, you shouldn't have but more importantly you shouldn't be in my house." I hiss this at him quietly. I don't want Colton or Johnny to hear us.

He understands and whispers back, "Technically you said not to call you. You didn't say not to come over."

I gape at him and am in disbelief that he is nearly smirking at me!

"Are you being serious right now?" I glare at him out of the corner of my eye while I refill my mug. To stall, I take a couple of sips of the steaming liquid and feel it moving through my chest toward my belly.

"I'm sorry, really, Dixie, I am." He sits in one of the bar chairs and looks up at me through his eyelashes. Dear Lord, I pray, please help me resist this man's charms!

"You have nothing to be sorry about, Mason. Really. We got caught up in the moment. That kind of dancing can do that to you, and I knew that, and I went anyway." I hang my head and shake it. "I knew you had a woman in your life already, but I obviously needed the reminder."

"But that's just it, Dixie. I don't have a woman in my life. Not in the way you think." He lifts my chin and makes sure that I am listening. "But I do have to think about the way the public finds that out, and I promised her she could decide how it should go down."

"I don't want you to make this change because of me. I'm not ready for that sort of pressure or commitment."

"No. I promise you this was in the works for a long time. Our whole relationship was designed by the studio for maximum publicity. We get along great, and

I respect her, but she's ten years younger than me for crying out loud."

"That's nothing for a Hollywood couple." I say because I don't want to let him off this easy.

"I can't argue that." He runs his hand through his hair, and it seems as though he is trying to gather his thoughts. Then he looks around to where his brother and nephew are working. "I should be helping them. Can we talk more later?"

I consider this for a few seconds but then decide to go for it. After all, I still have lots to tell him.

"Sure. Come by around eight o'clock tonight if you're free. Bring some wine or whiskey. Whichever you prefer."

"Thank you." He breathes then goes and joins in on hanging the warehouse door that he found for me.

I go and sit at the piano and start playing the "Sinner's Prayer," offering some noise and entertainment for the crew.

When they leave at two that afternoon, I am exhausted and head out to the porch for a nap in my swinging bed.

Thirty One

I wake up just before six that night. The air has gotten chilly, and I snuggle farther under the down comforter. I start praying earnestly for guidance, wisdom, and strength to get through this night and the truths that need to be spoken. I also pray that Mason would be able to understand my perspective.

Because I know we will be having drinks later, I warm up some crusty French bread and throw some Klamath and giant green olives and garlic in the ninja and make some spread.

After eating, I go and wash my face and braid my hair. I'm as plain as I can get, and I even pull on some sweats and an old Arkansas Razorback T-shirt.

At eight o'clock sharp, there is a knock on the front door. I open it, and Mason comes in, carrying a plain brown bag, which he sits on the counter. He is wearing an equally old pair of jeans and a BHS sweatshirt. It seems as though we are playing from the same handbook.

I pull a bottle of Jameson Signature Reserve out of the bag and raise my eyebrows at him.

"I got it at LAX on my return flight. I was hoping you would like it."

"Absolutely, it's sweeter and more floral than the Gold Reserve because they use American oak and Spanish cherry to store it in versus the virgin oak for the Gold. Equally good, but different." I look up, and he is looking so intently at me it unsettles me.

"Anyway, never mind about all that. Let's get to the more important question: on the rocks or with a mixer?"

"On the rocks, please."

I pour two high boys and bring them to the couch, where he sits on one side, and I sit at the other. We both sip our drinks in silence for a bit while we listen to the music playing in the background. I have a playlist going on the Bose system, and Miles Davis is at his smoothest playing "So What."

I decide to break the ice. "I think I understand what you were saying earlier about you and Hanna, but I need to be sure. If you don't mind, that is."

He looks down into his glass and sighs. "Being part of Hollywood is all I ever wanted. Every since that first year in drama club at BHS, I felt that once I succeeded there, my life would be perfect and fulfilled. And in a way, I was right. I absolutely love what I am doing. Acting is in my blood. But I found out early that there is a loss of freedom that goes with it, and not just the paparazzi following you around, but the expectations that the studio people and your own managers put on you." He frowns a little and then looks up at me. "What you said last night about power. There's a lot of truth to that, but at the same time, we are some of the most powerless people in the business. Public opinion can make or break you, and perception is absolutely

141

reality. So you wear the latest trends, you spend hours on your looks, you go to all the right places, and well, you date the right people." He winces a little but then his forehead clears. "However, there has been a shift the last few years. Twitter and Facebook have changed the way actors can get in touch with their fans. You can be a little more real and control the tone of what they hear about you." He looks at me for a couple of seconds, and I indicate he should go on.

"Dix, this thing with Hanna was brought on by a poll on *Shipwrecked*'s fan page. They asked who would you most like to see a real-life relationship between amongst the characters. And then *bam!* Three months later, the studio has us making public appearances together." He looks down into his glass and runs his finger around and around the edge as he seems to be thinking about how he wants to continue.

"We do have great chemistry together, which made it very believable, but we quickly figured out that it ended there. We have very little in common. I'm very private, and she loves the camera. I'm a bleeding heart, and she finds my causes boring. Hell, she finds me boring."

"How do you feel about her, Mase?"

He starts to speak and then hesitates. I take a deep sip of my drink as I wait for the answer.

"She's very beautiful of course, and she's very energetic and youthful. She's a sweet girl, but she has a lack of focus and lives in the moment. I'll admit when we first starting showing up as a couple I thought that we may actually end up making a go of it. I wasn't capable at the time of feeling anything beyond the surface, but I liked being with her, and at the time, it felt like it might be enough."

"What changed?" I ask because I really do want to know.

"Simple. You walked into my brother's shop. That's what changed. The passion for Johnny's art came screaming out of you, and when you spoke, I could tell you were more than just a little intelligent. You had this depth and a touch of sadness, and then you told me where you lived and I just wanted—no, I *had* to get to know you. So then I show up and see what you did to the cottage, knowing that it means you spent weeks shut away in that house, working on something you were passionate about that you were doing to impress no one but yourself, bringing your vision to reality. That was so refreshing to me—the fact that you could care less what was going on in the world, didn't care what you might be missing, and who might be missing you." He smiles that smile at me, and I flush. He grins and then keeps talking, "Then we sat and talked that night, and you were so interested in my childhood stories and never once mentioned my present. I just felt so normal and challenged by your intellect. Being with you reminded me that I am not always the most interesting person in the room. Not even close."

"I don't know about that. I find you very interesting, Mason. I just think you have forgotten that your job is a teeny, tiny part of who you are."

He chuckles and leans his head against the back cushion of the couch. He crunches on a piece of ice and then says, "I *had* forgotten that, but not anymore. Now

I understand. When I was out in LA this past week, I felt like I was on a business trip instead of at home. I couldn't wait to get back here."

He stretches out his legs and entwines them with mine. I start to get a panicky feeling about where this conversation is going.

"You see, the day before I left, I met with the show producers and Hanna, and we discussed a breakup. I'm the bad boy on the show, so it's natural that I be the one to be the villain, so they'll fabricate something to that affect and release it."

"So if that's the case, why did you get so angry last night? Wouldn't those pictures leaking to the press be a good way to end it?"

He purses his lips and says, "Yes, I suppose it would have been, but two things: we agreed no one would get blindsided, and second, I would never allow you to be associated with something considered anything close to sordid." He looks at me and then adds, "The reason I was so mad was because the guy interrupted something I wanted so bad." I gulp, and I feel my face go deep red, and I look down.

"I mean, seriously, Dixie. The way you dance"— he blows out a big breath and closes his eyes—"I was desperate to hold you."

While his eyes are closed, I take in every curve and hollow on his face. I memorize the shadow of his beard, and the sweetheart curve of his upper lip. His eyebrows and eyelashes are so dark that they are a startling contrast even against his tanned skin. I feel my heart swell and then start to break. I think I am falling fast in love with him, and I know I am about to jeopardize it all.

I get up from the couch and walk into the kitchen. His eyes follow me as I stop to refill my drink. The kitchen island is between us, and I lean over and rest on my forearms as I start to speak.

"Mason, before we move forward any further with this, I need to tell you about me. About what brought me here. I have to be completely honest with you because I am feeling things for you that I never thought I would." I take a deep breath, and my heart continues to break at the way his face lights up over what I just said.

"Three years ago, I had two unthinkable tragedies happen in short order. I blamed two men directly for these—one was my husband." I see the confusion begin on is face. "He let his pride, ego, and ambition get in the way of doing what was right, and it hurt so many people you can't even imagine." I take a deep draw of my whiskey to settle my stomach, which has started to churn. "The second man was utterly enraged by the outcome of husband's action and took his anger out on me. That led to me being attacked and nearly killed." I take a deep shuddering breath and say, "And my daughter *was* killed."

I hear him gasp, and I hate what's coming.

"After I recovered physically, I secluded myself at a location outside of the country. I went into total isolation and began my struggle against the anger, pain, and betrayal I felt. The hatred was white-hot and started eating me up from the inside like a cancer. I couldn't think of anything else for the first few months.

I cried so much that my face was chapped and red and peeling, and I lost so much weight that the friend who was letting me use his property became physically ill when he came to visit me one day. That shook me a little but also got me to thinking about the future. Did I want to go back? Back to work, back to my friends and family, back to the mess that was left behind."

I sip my drink again and lean back against the counter. "At first, the answer was no, and I began planning my suicide." His head pops up at this point, and I close my eyes rather than look at the emotion coming from his. "I made a list of all the ways I could do it without anyone knowing. Not that I was ashamed. I just didn't want to give my husband's family or the other man the satisfaction. I had things on the list like, falling off an ocean-side cliff, drowning in the rip tide, falling on the deck of the pool, and drowning. You name it, I thought of it. Each day, I would get up and set out on trial runs, and each day, something happened to keep me from doing it." I am pacing now, going around the kitchen island in slow circles. This is very painful for me to say out loud.

"The day that I was going to explore falling off the cliff, I was sitting on a large rock on the edge, looking down into the churning surf below when a little old man walked up and sat down beside me. He asked what I was doing, and for some reason I told him the truth. He just nodded and started crying. It took me completely by surprise, and I asked him why he cared, he didn't know me. And he told me that it didn't matter because I was one of God's children, and he knew that God was very sad when one of his children were hurting. We talked for a while about my anger and about forgiveness. He told me I could have peace again. He promised me, took my face in his hands, and promised me I could. And I believed him. He gave me a book before he left, and I went home and read it, every word. It was the *New Testament*. I had been in church most of my young life, Mace, and I had never read it all the way through." I am amazed anew at this fact, and I shake my head in remembrance. I look at Mason, and I can see he still hasn't put the story together.

"I got better every day. My hope and optimism returning little by little each day. The overwhelming theme of what I was reading seemed to be forgiveness. I came to understand that the only hope I had of leading a normal life was to be able to forgive those two men, and I mean, not just be able to say it; really, really mean it." I stop again and grab a Kleenex to dab my eyes.

"I was able to forgive my husband. He was a weak man who had been a slave to his addictions. His final mistake had caused his death, so he had paid the ultimate price. Also while I hated the things he stood for in the end, at one time I knew him to be brilliant and caring. Finally, his flaws had been bred into him from an early age by a proud, arrogant family." I give little shrug. "I guess what I am saying is that because I knew him so well, it was easier for me to forgive him completely."

I draw in a deep breath and plunge forward. "The second man was harder. Because, while he wasn't directly responsible for the harm to me and my daughter, he had acted on assumptions and suppositions and made himself judge, jury, and executioner, and in truth, he had everything wrong, and my daughter paid the price for his ignorance." Tears are streaming down my face now, and I see his face has turned red. He is feeling anger on my behalf, but the fact that his eyes won't meet mine says he is thinking about his own demons. Finally he looks up at me.

"Did you? Were you able to forgive that monster?"

"Yes. It took another whole year of praying and finally forgiving myself for the role I had played in the whole situation, but God put a plan on my heart to get there. I listened, followed through, and now I am in a place that I never could have imagined. You know, a wise woman told me recently that God performs His biggest miracles in the midst of tragedies. I am a firm believer in that now." I can see that I have his attention, and I think the truth is starting to niggle in his brain.

"You see, Mason, God not only brought me to a place where I have forgiven this man, I've fallen in love with him."

The truth dawns on his face, and I watch him go through from being confused to stunned to devastation. He then crumples in on himself, and I rush over to him and wrap my arms around him. He is shaking with sobs, and this goes on for a full five minutes.

"Shhhhh, Mason, please. Don't do this to yourself." I crawl into his lap and rock back and forth with him. "Please, Mason, I talked to Sandy, and she told me how you grieved. Please understand that I really do forgive you."

He finally looks up at me and searches my eye. He blinks and rubs his hand over his face. He starts to talk and stops. Then he starts again, "You changed your name. You were Rexanna Beauregard then."

"Yes, it was so I could get the press off my back. Dixie is my middle name, and Bryan is my maternal grandparents' last name. They raised me most of my life."

He moans and lays his head on my chest. "I could never, never express enough to you how sorry I am. I had no idea that those people...that they would do what they did."

"I know, Mason. And I know that you were in a bad place when all that was going on. I even understand your anger. I was very angry with David and NWM and the others involved back then as well." I run my fingers through his hair. He looks up at me and his eyes are red and wet and he looks like a little boy. My heart is breaking for him, but for myself as well.

"I didn't know, Dixie, I didn't really know anything about you. I found out later about the work you were doing, and I just...I was horrified. And then when I tried to find you later, I learned about the foundation you set up with the settlement. You can't imagine how much I have hated myself since then." I am watching his face, and I become alarmed when I see the anger settling into his features. I don't want him to go backward.

"Meeting you in the shop was the first time I was able to fully forget all that and start thinking about a future—with you." He chuckles and then cries a little more. He looks up at me and shakes his head. "What kind of sick irony is that?"

I am crying now, and he sits back and looks at me. He touches the scar that runs along my jaw and the one that runs from my ear down to my collar bone. "I wanted to ask about these scars so many times," he says. Then he looks questioningly into my eyes, and I nod. I have decided he can have full reign with my heart and body and mind.

He reaches down and pulls my shirt up and touches the thick ropes of scars that emanate from a center point just under my ribcage on the right side. He traces the entire length of each of them and kisses the point where they all come together. I shudder with a swallowed sob because there is finality in the kiss. When he is done, he looks up at me with sorrow and regret.

"I...I can't...I'm sorry," he is whispering as he says these words. Then he gets up from the couch and walks past me. I stare straight ahead at the beautifully framed canvas I bought at his brother's shop, and when I hear the door swing shut, I flinch, bury my head in my arms, and give in to the grief I've only scratched the surface of.

Thirty Two

The next morning, I crawl out of bed with puffy eyes and a pounding headache. I shower and scrape my hair back, throw on a jersey dress, and head out to church.

I sing but not with my usual gusto. I am probably close to a state of shock and am moving on cruise control.

When the service is over, I make my way to the back, but Ms. Sally Charles stops me before I leave.

"Child, I want you to come home with me today. I want to have a proper Sunday dinner, and some needed fellowship with another child of God."

My first inclination is to decline as my mood is not one to share with company. But I feel a very strong urge coming from within to say yes. So I do.

"I would be honored, Ms. Sally. I will even help cook if you trust me."

We make our way out the front door and across the street to a cute little bungalow that is pristine white with black shutters and a screened-in front porch. The landscaping is immaculate, and I feel certain that Pastor White and the men of the church are responsible for it. I feel like all I've done for twelve hours is cry, but suddenly, I am crying again. There is just so much kindness in the world if you pay attention.

We go inside, and Ms. Sally starts directing me around the kitchen. I am apparently going to be making a crawfish pot pie. When I am finally finished with all the ingredients and stick the pie in the oven for the forty-five minutes it will take to bake, she asks me to sit with her at the table with some ice-cold sweet tea.

"Now, my dear, please tell me what is troubling you so much."

I take a deep breath and blow it out as I look out the kitchen window at the robin-egg blue sky. I know that it is going to hurt, but I want to tell this amazing, wise woman. So I do. I tell her everything about Mason and me.

Just as I am finishing up, the buzzer goes off, and I jump up to get the pie out of the oven. Ms. Sally tells me where to find the bowls and forks, and I serve us both up a heaping helping.

While we are waiting for the meal to cool off just a bit, Ms. Sally starts talking.

"Child, what you have told me is a really difficult situation. You've seen and felt God's forgiveness and passed it on to another of his children. That's a very special thing, young lady. But as I see it, the problem is in your young man's inability to forgive his self."

"Yes, it is. I knew it would likely happen, Ms. Sally, but I had no choice. I couldn't carry on in our relationship if he didn't know."

"I can see that, dear. And you are right, but just because you are able to think that clearly doesn't mean he can just yet. You've had months to plan what you need or want to do and have followed that plan with a one-track mind. Your Mason just had a bomb dropped on him."

She is right, of course.

"Dixie, dear, you need to think back to when you first decided that forgiveness was your path. How did you feel, and how long did it take you to get there?"

What about that? Am I going to have to wait a whole year for him to be able to forgive himself? Because that's how long it took me.

She goes on, "The way I see it, dear, you need to turn to the one who got you through your mess. He listens, and He knows our hearts, and He knows your young man's heart. You need to let God rule the situation, and you need to be prepared to accept His answer no matter what it is. After all, sweetie, you got what you came here for. Am I right? You have forgiven Mr. Mason McCoy? Falling in love was not part of the original plan was it?"

That smacked me between the eyes like a frying pan.

Thirty Three

When I pull up at my house, I spot Sandy sitting on the front porch steps. When she spots my car, she stands and waits for me to walk up. I open the door and wave her in. I know in the pit of my stomach that she is here with bad news, and I brace myself.

"Sandy. I would say it's good to see you, but—"

"I can understand that."

"I assume you are here because of Mason?"

"Yes." She looks uncomfortable and doesn't seem to know what to do with her hands. Finally, she pulls an envelope out of her purse and lays it on the counter. "I told him I didn't want to do this. I told him that he should come talk to you himself. But the McCoy brothers come by stubborn honestly." She walks over to the window and looks out.

"Is he gone?" I ask. It's like ripping a Band-Aid off—better to get it over with quick.

"Yes, he left this morning. He was going to LA for a couple of weeks. He has some camera work to do for *Shipwrecked*. After that, I'm not sure." She looks at me then and shrugs. "He made me promise to bring that letter to you and tell you that he needs to 'work things out.'" She actually uses her fingers to make quote marks.

154

"Do you think I'll see him again, Sandy?"

"I don't know, dear. I really just don't know. I think the one thing he was sure of in his life is that when he caught up with Rexanna Beauregard, he would finally receive the wrath he felt he deserved. I think he can't move on until that happens. Having you not only forgive him but love him upset his world view and everything he believed in." She walks over and puts her hand on my arm. "He said that you held him like a child and comforted him." Her voice breaks on the last couple of words, and she looks from eye to eye. "Can I assume that means you have truly forgiven him?"

I absorb everything she has said and roll it around my brain for a second. Finally, I nod once, and she smiles a brief, bittersweet smile.

"Then read that letter, Dixie. It may help, or it may not. But I know he spent a lot of time on it." She gives me a sly little look and goes on, "I also wrote his e-mail address on the outside of the envelope. It's the one he uses in the business."

"Thank you, Sandy. You are a really good sister-in-law." She gives me a tight hug and then changes the subject.

"Give me your sign up sheet for Glee Club, Dixie. I'll get it posted tomorrow, and you can be taking auditions by the end of the week. I'm guessing you'll welcome the distraction."

I can't help but feel a tiny bit of gratefulness for this, and I salute and say, "Yes, boss," before going over to my desk and getting the sheets for her.

Thirty Four

It's two weeks until Christmas, and I am working with the Glee Club on a short program to perform at the Christmas-tree lighting across from the Hancock Community Building. I hadn't been expecting to have the group perform this quickly, but there really is some amazing talent in the group.

My star performer is Colton McCoy. The boy is an incredibly talented piano player and has an achingly poignant singing voice. He does great on the 50s and 60s versions of "White Christmas" and "Little Drummer Boy." I adapted the versions to fit him even better, and the result is pure magic. The other surprising star is a young man named Peter who is built like a linebacker, and probably, the shyest person I've ever encountered. But something comes over the kid when the music starts. His voice is a clear bass. When I first heard his voice, I immediately thought of Geoff Tate and Queensryche. For the program, I have him singing an Elvis-style version of "Santa Claus Is Coming to Town."

My biggest hurdle to the club is the amount of untalented female applicants. I understand that this is because the amount of cute boys that applied, but it meant weeding out the ones who aren't musically gifted. There has been some wailing and gnashing of teeth, but it came down to just five talented girls out of twenty-five applicants. Jaci, who is a freshman and a tiny little fireplug, has a growly, soulful voice like Tracy Chapman. I love her passion. Sarah has a clear voice with a range like Mariah Carey. She is pretty, preppy and undisciplined. I am very excited about her potential. Jenna is sweet and shy and has a powerhouse voice that reminds me of Celine Dion. Deanna is most comfortable with the country-Western-style, and I love how committed she is. Finally, there is Kim, and she gives me goose bumps when she sings. She can slay any blues, jazz, or soul song I throw at her. She's a junior, but her soul is fifty years older. I absolutely cannot wait for the Christmas event so these kids can show how talented they are.

Thirty Five

It was Thanksgiving before I had been able to read Mason's letter. I had a lovely dinner thanks to Michelle and Bob, who had taken pity on me and invited me for lunch at Michelle's family's house. It was crazy and chaotic with kids running all over. In other words, it was perfect. We had turkey, oyster dressing, and pumpkin pie. I enjoyed every second, and when I got home late that evening, I took the letter and sat down to read it and drink a glass of wine.

I read it about five times, and went through being angry with him, sorry for him, and missing him. In the end, the words weren't important; what was behind them was. He doesn't feel he is worthy of the forgiveness I have offered. He is hanging on to what happened in the past and using it to keep from opening himself up to the love he wants, and I need to give to him. He's gone to his home in Malibu and then will be making the Agent Guerin movie, followed by several weeks in the Caribbean, filming the television show. He didn't say good-bye, just said that he would be in touch when he could.

After I read it, I sat for a while, thinking of how much I was hurting and how it was a familiar feeling to have this huge knot in my chest, but it was very different than before. I had no anger this time.

I was also struck by how I had been the same as Mason when it came to accepting God's forgiveness. I kept throwing my past in and refusing to believe He could forgive my mess. I was so lucky that He was relentless in letting me know how much He loved me through His Word—wait—through His Word. That thought gave me an idea; I reached over and grabbed the envelope from the letter, and there, printed in Sandy's neat hand mrm@job.net. I turned on my tablet and fired up my e-mail.

> Dear Mason,
>
> I hope things are going well where you are. Things are good here. I had Thanksgiving dinner with Michelle and Bob. They are an amazing couple, and their families are so much fun. It was great of them to take me in. I had forgotten what it was like to celebrate a holiday with a big, unruly family.
>
> I've been taking auditions for the Bay High Glee Club, and I think it's going to be epic! There is a ton of talent here. I have two piano players, a drummer, four guitar players, one who can play sax, and three violinists. There are some singing stars in there, as well. Chief among them is your nephew, Colton. He is a gem, and I am so lucky to have him. I hope someday you get to see him in action. You will be so proud!
>
> Mason, I miss you. I wasn't kidding when I said I had fallen in love with you. I know you

may not feel the same, and that's okay. But I at least need you to be my friend again, when you are ready. To do that, you need to know that what I said about forgiving you was the truth. I don't think even I realized it was true until I said it out loud in that moment. It took years, and I had the advantage of knowing who you were. I set out to forgive you, Mason. Just so I could move on with my life. I had no idea all the rest would happen. I know it's hard, but please believe me.

By the way, as soon as you get the chance, please look up Matthew 18:21–35. It will help you understand where I started my journey.

Warm regards,
Dixie

In the two weeks since I wrote that e-mail, I have written eight more e-mails, telling him about the happenings in Bay St. Louis and how the Glee Club is progressing. Every time I include a new scripture on forgiveness. Each one is a message that I worked through myself during my exile. I haven't gotten any answers, but that hasn't dampened my spirit.

Thirty Six

The day of the Christmas tree lighting dawns bright and a little chilly. December in the Bay is incredibly pleasant with chilly nights and days in the upper 60s to low 70s. I head down to the courthouse a few hours early to help with the decorating and set up. Michelle meets me there. Her company donates the lights and ornaments for the tree every year, and she has such fabulous taste that everyone relies on her for guidance in the actual decorating.

For lunch, we walk down the block to a fun little coffee shop for a salad and some warm apple cider.

"So sugar, what are y'all doing for Christmas? Are you going back home?" she asks.

"No, I don't have any immediate family left back there. My aunt and uncle are all that's left, and as much as they would welcome me, it's still a little awkward."

"Then why don't you come with me and Bob again? We loved having you with us at Thanksgiving!" I smile at the memories of that event.

"That means a lot to me, Michelle. It really does. But Christmas is different and much more intimate. I think I'll go over and stay in New Orleans for a few

161

days and serve some meals with the local food bank. It'll do me some good."

"You are such a good person, Dixie."

"Not really. I get as much or more from it than they do. Truth be told, it reminds me of how good I really do have it and that I shouldn't take it for granted."

"Well, I don't care what you say, girl. I think you are awesome. Now, let's pay the check so we can go whip this event into the party we all need."

Thirty Seven

Mason,

The Christmas-tree lighting was tonight. Oh how I wish you had been here. I know Sandy recorded it for you, and I hope you get an idea of how magical it was. Everyone was so happy and full of cheer, and the kids did so good that I cried like a proud mama. We called the performance Christmas through the Ages, and we started with some blues era, went into the rock-n-roll period, the Crooners, country, and ended with some contemporary pop. I have so much excitement for what this class is going to bring in the future. I'm only sad that Colton is a junior and not a freshman.

Speaking of Colton, I have started working with him on an admission packet and audition for Julliard. Johnny and Sandy are behind him all the way, and I feel like his potential has been barely tapped. We are working on some original music, and he has real aptitude for it.

Well, Christmas is coming up, and I am going to spend it in New Orleans. I have some good friends there that also don't have close family, and we have our own little "Island of Misfit Toys" dinner on the traditional holidays.

Also through my foundation, I support a meal kitchen in the ninth ward. I am going to go help out delivering Christmas dinners to those who are homebound. I'm looking forward to it. I learn so much and am blessed every time I go. I hope you get to spend Christmas with the ones you love too.

I have a gift for you. It's for Christmas, obviously, which is my favorite holiday because it seems to bring out the kindness in people. I also love the Christmas lights and decorations. And I love you, Mason. I really miss talking to you so much. The debates about music, and books, food, and wine, well, they've been terrific. You are my favorite person to talk to, truly.

Your friend,
Dixie

P.S. I gave in and picked up the *Harry Potter* books. You were right. They were fantastic. But I'm not sure I'm ready to give J.K. Rowling Roald Dahl's crown just yet.

The morning of Christmas Eve I go for a run down to the French Market and along Front Boulevard until I reach Canal. Here I stop and go down to the riverfront and find a bench to sit on. I watch some ships go by and wonder where they are going and what they are delivering. I empty my mind and pray, again, for Mason to find forgiveness. I pray also for the country, and especially the communities I am part of, to be captivated by the special spirit of Christmas that brings peace, love, and charity.

I have been at my flat for a few days and plan to stay through the following Friday. I want a full weekend at home for last-minute preparations for moving into full-time teaching. I have been invited to a dinner party nearly every night between then and now. I've accepted most, including one tonight at Randy and Paul's Garden District mansion. I am happy to see them and their newly renovated house. I have some delicious wine to take and some gingerbread cookies that I made the night before.

I get up and set out down Canal Street toward Royal to complete my circuit. My headphones are pumping out some upbeat music by Pink, and I settle into a good rhythm. As I'm passing the JW Marriott, I spot a familiar dark head coming out of the lobby to get into the back of a dark SUV. For split second our eyes meet, and then he is inside and the vehicle is pulling away.

I stumble to a stop and stare after it until it turns. I guess I knew that he might be spending time in New Orleans when the new movie got under way, but I am shocked that he is here *now*. I turn back and look at the front of the hotel. He didn't have any luggage, so maybe he's staying here another night. That gives me an idea.

Thirty Eight

That evening I take a lot of time with my hair and put on stockings and a little black A-line dress. Paul and Randy like their dinners to be on the formal side, mostly for the theatrical feeling that comes with it. Luckily, I have a chic pair of low-heeled black boots that are quite comfortable. I wouldn't be able to stand heels all night.

For a final touch, I wrap a copper silk scarf around my neck and put on some diamond drop earrings. I carry the wine and cookies in a lovely Parisian print tote and take them down to the Audi. I have also tucked a small but elegantly wrapped gift into my bag. I plan to drop by the JW and leave it at the front desk, provided Mason is actually staying there.

Walking into the lobby, I walk up to the youngest male I can find and hope that my makeup and hair will do its trick and make him want to help me, as well as hope that he's not gay.

He's not, and it does.

"Hi, uh, Brad," I say as I read his name tag. "I hope you can help me because my rear is on the line. I've made a dreadful mistake, and I need to see if I can correct it." I put on what I hope is a flirty pout, and I can see his chest puff a little at the potential of being my white knight. "You see, I have this gift that I was supposed to hand-deliver to Mason McCoy yesterday afternoon. It's from my boss, and she will be extremely ticked if I don't get it to him." I stop and blow a breath through my bangs to give the impression of being exasperated at my demanding boss. "Can you tell me if he's still here? If he is, I can just leave it with you to deliver to him."

He looks at me with a raised eyebrow. "Who's your boss?" he asks.

"Well, she lives here part time with her equally famous husband and their six kids."

"You mean—" and his hand unconsciously gestures toward his lips.

"Yes, that is exactly who I mean."

"Wow. Well, yes, I can make sure he gets it. Mr. McCoy is indeed staying here tonight."

I hand him the small-silver paper wrapped gift. Inside is an iPod that contains several playlists that I put together based upon our many musical discussions, including one that I believe is representative of Special Agent Guerin.

I walk out happy that I will at least have made this contact with him.

Paul opens the door when I arrive a few minutes later. He is wearing a beautiful Santa hat that has mistletoe hanging from the white fluffy ball on the end. He pulls me into an embrace.

"Miss Bryan, I do declare you are a sight for sore eyes!" He leans back from me and his eyes dance. "Love what you've done with that hair!" I smile back at him and kiss him on the cheek.

"Your opinion means heaps to me, Paul, so I'm very glad you like this." I hand him the tote as Randy comes around the corner and grabs me into a hug. I feel at home with these two men, who became my great friends during my early days in New Orleans. They are enormously wealthy, but the only way you would know is their penchant for fixing up grand old homes. They are two of the most charitable men you'll ever meet and love picking up what they call *strays*; in other words, people like me. I can't wait to see who shows up to this dinner.

"OMG, Randy! Dixie has brought us four bottles of that Mathis Grenache we had at her flat." Paul reveals this as he is digging in the tote. "Double OMG, she made her infamous orange-glazed gingerbread cookies too!" Now he is squealing like a teenage girl. Randy and I look at each other and giggle.

"Well, don't just stand there. Go put the wine in the cooler. I am dragging this gorgeous Amazon into the living room to play me some music!" With that, Randy literally pulls me by my hand into their grand parlor to a fabulous white grand piano.

"What'll it be tonight?" I ask. Randy has a great voice and loves to sing. He generally drags me into a duet.

"Let's start with 'Merry Christmas, Baby.' I'm in an Elvis mood."

I start playing and sing with him on the chorus. I love this joyful singing, and for the first time in weeks, I am able to forget how much I miss Mason.

While we launch into "Baby, It's Cold Outside," the doorbell rings, and we wave at Cindy, Marsha, and Dale—the gang from Funky Pirate. Cindy has been a lifesaver for me. She recognized my need to play with the band and never questioned why. This is one of the things I love about this city; people don't judge and don't pry. They just accept your eccentricities and go on.

They gather around the piano, and we all start singing "The Christmas Song." The next time the doorbell rings, Paul runs to get it, but I can't see the door because of the group around me. Dale has just talked me into playing and singing "The House of the Rising Sun." I told him that it wasn't very seasonal, but he said it was his favorite, and it would be my gift to him. Well that and some of the cookies.

I love the song, as well, and put my best blues spin on it and enjoy it to the fullest. I tend to sing with my eyes closed, so when the song was done and the last note wrung out, I opened my eyes and gasped.

Thirty Nine

M ason was there. Standing at the end of the piano next to Paul and three people I didn't know. One was a stout older man with a bald head and an impressive goatee then a very fit man in his forties with thick, wavy Robert Redford type of hair. The other was a stunning woman with deep-red hair and ice-blue eyes. She was looking straight at me in a way that was incredibly unsettling.

The sudden silence hung in the air for a beat before Paul clapped his hands together. "We have some special guests with us tonight, gang!" He beams around at all of us and puts his hand on the arm of the bald man. "One of the areas that Randy and I have dabbled in for years is producing movies. We especially work on projects that can be filmed here in the New Orleans area. Well, Oscar here came to us with the idea of turning Bartholomew's delicious book series into a movie." Now he gestures to the Redford hair man. I am stunned. Randy and Paul are the ones financing the Agent Guerin movies?

I look from them to Mason, and he is staring directly at me. I smile, but he keeps the same expression. I'm not sure what to make of this, but Randy interrupts my thoughts by going on with the introductions.

"These two beautiful people you may recognize. Mason McCoy is going to play Agent Guerin, the main character, and Julia Thomas will play his wife, Ilene." He turns toward the rest of us. "And these are our dearest friends. We have the best dinner parties, you'll see! This is Cindy, she owns the Funky Pirate, the best little jazz bar in town. This is her beau, Dale, who besides having great taste in women also has great taste, period. He owns the World Renowned Culinary Arts School. Next is Marsha, she's the bartender at Cindy's bar. Marsha also speaks four languages, has lived in six countries, and has the most fascinating string of lovers in her past." He wriggles his eyebrows, and we all laugh. Then he turns to me. Yikes.

"And this is Dixie Bryan, who came out of nowhere last year. She has the most mysterious background of us all. She has degrees in things I can't pronounce, gives away a seemingly unending source of money at an alarming rate, sings like she was born in the forties as a black woman, and is, inexplicably, a very close friend to our good friend, Don Miguel, the president of Costa Rica!" He looks at me with his eyes round as silver dollars and says, "I swear we will get that out of you someday!"

I just laugh and wink at him and slide a glance over at Mason. His eyebrows are furrowed, and I wonder if he will let on that we know each other. I decide to let him take the lead on that decision.

Everyone is shaking hands and starting to break the ice. Randy and Paul look very pleased, and I start playing quietly to make background noise.

"Are you playing 'New York State of Mind'?" Surprised, I look up, and it's the author, Bartholomew Hight.

"Guilty." I say with a smile. "Please, have a seat." He slides in next to me on the piano bench, and I continue playing. "I want to tell you that I am a massive fan of your books, Mr. Hight."

"Please, call me Bart, madam." I laugh a little at that.

"Okay, Bart, but only if you'll return the favor and call me Dixie." I sneak a glance up at Mason and see that he is talking to Marsha and his fellow actor, Julia.

"You got it, Dixie. I'm very happy to hear you like the books."

"Oh, like is too soft of a word. I really do love them. In fact, I've got the biggest crush on Agent Guerin that may be bordering on obsession."

He chuckles, and we launch into an intense character discussion around his last couple books, and I am fascinated with how his mind works and some of the bizarre ways he comes up with his inspiration. We talk for more than a half hour before Paul announces that dinner is ready, and we reluctantly get up and go into the dining room.

The room is grand and intimate at the same time. There are library panels around the lower half of the room, which are stained the same light walnut as the floors. The upper portion of the room is painted a deep, dusky purple, and there is a breathtaking chandelier centered over the table that throws shadow and light over the whole space. The art that covers the wall is deeply and uniquely New Orleans in style. The chairs are all mismatched and come from local antique stores. You can imagine the history that exists behind them, which makes them priceless. The table and the side buffet are in the Louis XIV style with ball and claw feet.

As we sit, I notice four decanters of wine are placed along the table and a few waiters appear from nowhere and begin pouring the wine and placing salads in front of us. The lights are at half strength, and soon enough, the conversation and the wine begins flowing. The meal is a thing of beauty. A few of Dale's students came to prepare the dinner and have outdone themselves to impress their teacher. We have stuffed duck, beef tenderloin, and cornish hen to select from, as well as pommes frites, asparagus, and grilled zucchini strips to dip in the most amazing sauce I've ever tasted. Dessert is a mouthwatering assortment of sorbets—watermelon, grapefruit, and peppermint. During dinner, I am seated between Oscar and Julia and across from Mason. He seems to be doing everything he can to not make eye contact. Marsha is to one side and Paul on the other, and they seem to be doing a great job of keeping him in conversation. He's laughing and talking with them both, but I notice he seems to be consuming a large amount of wine, as well.

"So, Miss Dixie," Oscar leans into my line of sight "Randy tells us that you are a musical ingénue." I look over at Randy, and he raises his eyebrows.

"That's very nice of him, but maybe a bit of an overstatement. It is true that I am a student of all kinds of music. I love everything about it."

"Tell me, what kind of music would you imagine Agent Guerin listening to?" This comes from Bart at the end of the table.

I feel my ears burning as I look down at my hands. This is exactly what I just delivered to Mason's hotel. And then I also can't believe I am discussing this with the author of my favorite books. I feel a little giddy.

"I personally imagine Aloysius as being very unrestricted in his musical taste. In other words, if it is good and complex and has meaning in his life, he will put in on his playlist." I look over, and Bart is smiling and nodding encouragement. "For example, I would expect a playlist containing Enya's Storms in Africa, the complete works of Thomas Tallis, some Bach concertos and cello suites, and Vivaldi's violin concerto." By now, I feel more eyes on me. I look down the table, and Randy is leaning back in his seat with a smug look. He loves to be right.

I go on, "I would also definitely expect some chanting Monks, but most of all, I would expect some great jazz- and blues-classics. After all, he is from New Orleans, so I would say some Thelonius Monk, Harry Connick Jr., Nat Cole, Muddy Waters, Buddy Guy, and Hugh Laurie."

That one catches Oscar off guard. "Hugh Laurie? Is that the same guy as Dr. House?" He chuckles, and Julia smirks.

"You laugh, but he is also a gifted musician. In fact, I would put his version of 'St. James Infirmary' as second only to Louis Armstrong."

Bart is sitting back with his finger over his lips for a few seconds. "Would you consider being a musical consultant for the movie?" I am stunned at this question, but I immediately look across at Mason. He is looking into his glass of wine and swirling the contents around. I can tell he is very aware of our conversation, however.

"You will never know how flattered I am by you even asking, Mr. Hight, but I have my hands really full right now. I teach a music appreciation class and lead the Glee Club over in Bay St. Louis, Mississippi." I really am conflicted, but my first love is the school.

"Well, we wouldn't be doing the editing and sound until after most of the shooting is done. Could you give us some time this summer? We would make it worth your while." This is from Oscar. Before I can answer, he seems to be struck by a thought.

"Wait a minute, did you say Bay St. Louis?" Then he looks over at Mason, and my heart drops. "Mason, aren't you from that same town?" Now he, Julia, and Paul are looking intently between the two of us. "Do you know Dixie, Mason?"

Our eyes collide across the table and hold for a few seconds. I can tell that he is intoxicated, and yet, I let him take the lead. He is the one holding on to his anger, and I am done with mine. So the ball is in his court, so to speak. Suddenly, his eyes become hooded, and the smirk he is famous for shows up. I have a brief premonition of disaster, and then he opens his mouth.

"Why, yes, Oscar, I do know her although I know her best by her real name Rexanna Beauregard. Actually, we know each other very well." He winks at me then. I feel like throwing something at him. I look down the table at Paul and Randy and see the massive confusion cross their face.

"Wait what? Do you mean the Rexanna Beauregard that invented Algeater?" This is asked by Julia. I don't know which of us is more shocked. We all look at her, but she is squinting at me. I look around the table and make eye contact with all my friends before I answer.

"Yes, ma'am, that was me." I look past her to Paul. "Beauregard was my late husband's last name." He looks intrigued but not angry.

Now, Bart is sitting straight up in his chair and looking at me much more intently. "Are we talking about the Algeater that cleaned the Mississippi River after that waste plant explosion?" He turns and looks at Randy and says, "This has turned into a very memorable dinner party after all, my friend." He grins and turns back to me. "I would love it if you would give me a top-line description of this invention of yours. I heard about it on the news, but I never really understood how it worked."

"Well, it wasn't so much of an invention as it was a tweaking of nature. Algae already fed on specific waste by-products and produced oxygen. I just figured out how to manipulate the genetic structure to make the algae feed on human waste. Then, taking it one step further than that, I mutated a separate strain to feed on the chemical by-products. Once the feeding process is over, the new algae turns pink and can be harvested and used as a fuel."

"That's fascinating. I saw a few articles on you after the explosion and resulting contamination. I couldn't believe that someone so young had accomplished that." Then his forehead wrinkles, and he goes on, "I also seem to remember that the media went crazy a few weeks later over the story about how the young woman that created Algeater had been attacked and disappeared." Now he raises his eyebrow, and Cindy chimes in.

"That's right, I remember now." Her expression turns to one of shock. "Dear God, Dixie! Was that you? The woman that was blown up by those crazy environmentalists was you? That photo haunted my nightmares for weeks!"

Now everyone is talking over each other at once as the pieces of the story come together from their separate memories. I look across at Mason and I wonder what his reason could possibly be for exposing me. I know that eventually their memories will put the whole story together. He is staring back at me, and I can sense a bit of sorrow coming from him as if he is someone who has lit a fuse and has time to think about what's coming but is unable to stop it. I continue to hold his gaze until he lifts his glass and drains the wine in it. Just then, it clicks for Dale.

"Wait a minute," he bellows. "It was you. You were the one that got her killed!" He's looking straight at Mason. "Yeah, that's where I heard your name from—Mason McCoy. You were the one that got those people all riled up."

"Dale, he didn't kill me, I'm still here," I say.

"Don't try and protect me, Dixie. I did what he says," Mason speaks up, and the whole room goes deadly quiet. He looks around, and I can see this is what he was wanting the whole time—to lay his sins bare and let the world judge him. He stands now and leans against the back of the chair and looks right at me.

"Dixie's deceased husband was the drunken leader of the plant that exploded. He was too busy sleeping with the systems inspector to do his job right. His lax attitude towards the safety protocols caused the tragedy, and I blamed his pregnant wife." He looks around the table at each person and lets what he just said sink in. He stops on me.

"I dedicated several long, tirade-filled blogs to the theory that she was likely an unloving harpy that drove him to drink and probably wouldn't sleep with him after getting pregnant. I laid the entire responsibility for the nasty contamination of the Mississippi River at her feet and did everything I could to destroy her. I fired up the troops over the fact that she stood to gain millions from this disaster that she created." He never looks away. I am transfixed and barely blink even though my eyes are spilling streams of tears.

"Mason."

"Shut up, Dixie" he says, and I hear several gasps. "You can't save me from this." He swipes at his own eyes briefly. "When news of that stuffed bear exploding became news, I was brought out of my hate-filled stupor, and I actually looked into the woman herself. Imagine my surprise when I discovered that she had almost single-handedly saved the Gulf area I call home not destroyed it. That she had, in fact, won a Nobel Prize for her invention years earlier. An invention, by the way, that she had sold for less than half it's worth to a conglomerate of energy companies in exchange for the contracted requirement that they give one-third of all fuel created from the Algeater product to poor countries to help provide heating and electricity. Oh, and of the twenty-one billion dollars she received, she put 20.9 billion into a charitable trust to be given away." He shakes his head and rubs his temples with his fingers. "This was the woman that I had inspired a bunch of kids, whose biggest contribution to society is that they haven't reproduced to blow up, taking away any chance of her passing her magnificent genes to another generation."

I can feel the atmosphere changing with every word.

"So you would think she would hate me, right? She had every right to. I even tried to find her so she could hate me, hit me, and spit on me, but she took off; down to Costa Rica and Don Miguel whose country had benefitted greatly from her invention"—he looks over at Paul who looks at me—"so there's a mystery solved."

I give Paul a halfhearted smile. At least they know the truth of why Miguel called and asked them to look me up.

"I gave up looking after awhile, of course, because that's how I am. I flare up and then die down shallow." I close my eyes and shake my head because I know that is not true. When I open them, he is back to the sardonic look he had at the start. "So imagine my surprise when the woman I have been carrying on an intense flirtation with, and am even thinking of breaking up with Hanna Foster for, tells me that 'Guess what? I'm Rexanna Beauregard, and I forgive you, and I think I love you!' Surprise!" he says this in a mocking voice, and I feel it deep in my stomach. I feel my heart breaking and, while it is familiar, the feeling nearly makes my knees buckle. I look around, and I see anger on some faces and sympathy on others. The latter hurts worse.

"But, you know, Rexie, I've been rethinking this whole thing. All those sweet e-mails you've been sending, reminding me every day of how much you want me have made me think it could be good for me. Imagine the headlines, Woman Mason McCoy Blew Up In Love With Him, I mean the publicity and my stud meter would be off the charts."

"Mason, stop it." Bart has stood up and is advancing on him.

"Hey now, Bart, I know you aren't used to it yet, but this is how Hollywood operates. Nothing is real. Everything is for show. Besides, she would be getting what she wants. By forgiving me, she's sticking a knife in my gut. She could have a first-hand view to my misery for as long as we are together."

"Geez, Mason, you're a real jerk," Marsha says, and by now nearly everyone is standing, and I see Dale and Oscar inching closer to Mason, and I feel certain one of them may throw a punch eventually.

"Stop!" I command. Everyone freezes and looks over at me. "Don't you all see what he's doing? He's purposely trying to make you all hate him and take my

side. He doesn't feel he deserves my forgiveness and so
it makes him angry." I walk around the table to where
he is standing and lift my hand as if I'm going to slap
him. Just as I thought, instead of flinching, he sticks his
jaw out further. Instead, I take my outstretched hand
and use it to cup his jaw and run my thumb over his
lips. His eyes flutter shut and for a second, he leans his
face further into my palm. A single, solitary tear slips
from the corner of his eye.

"Mason, I want you to listen to me because I am
going to say this once more then never again. I forgive
you. Not for you, for me. I had to forgive you in order
to move on with my life. I was able to do that because
God sent the ultimate Savior to forgive us humans
even when we don't deserve it. He was my example,
and I struggled against it, but He was relentless, and
as soon as I truly wanted the forgiveness, it happened.
Just like that." I stop and take a deep breath and look
straight into his eyes. "But, Mason, falling in love
with you was a complete surprise. That happened
because of who you are, warts and all. I could list
many reasons, but it doesn't matter. What does matter
is that it won't make you a bad person if *you* don't love
me. I wish you would accept both my forgiveness and
God's forgiveness because you deserve to go on with
your life, fully and wholly. If you don't, *that* will break
my heart, because I have found out that you are an
amazing, giving person, and you deserve happiness."
Tears are streaming down his face now, but amazingly
enough I am dry-eyed.

"So do I, Mason, but no other person can give that to me. I am fully, totally, and happily in charge of my own happiness now."

I step closer and put my lips on his for a couple of beats then smile against them. When I pull away, he reaches for me, but I step out of his grasp.

"Good-bye, Mason. Good luck with the movie."

At the door, Randy pulls me into a tight hug. He is crying, and it touches my heart that I have such good friends.

"Stop, Randy. There's been enough of that to last years." I wipe his cheek and see Paul coming up behind him. He is also crying.

"Dixie, if I had any idea—"

"Hey, now, there was no way for you to know. It's not as if I was up front about all this."

"It wasn't necessary. Your past doesn't matter in this town. You know that."

"You guys still coming over tomorrow for present delivery?"

"We wouldn't miss it for the entire world. It's the highlight of our holiday. Now, be careful on the way home." They both hug me again, and I head out to the portico for the short drive home.

Forty

It takes until a week after I am back home in Bay St. Louis before the news hits regarding my true identity. Pictures show up of me, jogging down Beach Boulevard and also coming out of the school and getting into my Audi S5. I have no idea when they were taken, which disturbs me even more.

Two days after that, the phone calls asking for interviews begin. I call my lawyer and have him take care of all those, as well as to start making preemptive calls to let all potential media outlets that I won't be speaking to any of them.

I am worried about what may happen to disrupt the local community, but to my surprise, the town closes around me, Sandy, Johnny, and the kids. They vow to help us keep our privacy, and they do a great job.

The worst part is that it brings out Mason's part in the event all over again, and his bad boy status takes on a deeper edge. He does nothing to defend it either.

When I arrived back in town, the first people I went to were Michelle and Bob. I felt like they deserved to hear the truth from me. Sandy was going to take care of telling Johnny and Colton.

Bob was surprisingly calm while Michelle was very emotional. When I had laid it all out, including Mason's rejection of my forgiveness, Bob got up and came to sit by me. He took my hand and squeezed it.

"You are an inspiration, and obviously, an incredibly strong woman." He sighs and then says, "So I am going to ask you to please not give up on him. I understand that you have been hurt again by his rejection, but I know Mason. I know him almost as well as I know Michelle." At this he raises his head in her direction and smiles so sweetly. "We aren't that different, Mason and I. Both of us stubborn and stupid, holding onto our idea of justice, not understanding that by doing what we think is right, we are actually as wrong as we can get."

Something in his tone made a light go on in my head, and I look over at Michelle then down at her left hand. Thoughts of Mason fly out of my head as I bound over to hug her, and we start jumping up and down and laughing. Then I am crying because I am just so happy for them. Also because what Bob said has settled in that hopeful part of my heart.

Before I left them, I told Bob that I wasn't giving up on Mason, but that I wouldn't actively seek him out any longer. He understood that because we both know Mason needs time and space to work out his own issues.

Forty One

The next couple of months fly by. I am knee-deep in planning the spring gala performance by the Glee Club as well as helping Michelle plan her wedding. The two events will only be three weeks apart. Michelle wants an outdoor wedding, so it has to be early May before it gets too hot. I'll never forget the day she came to me to discuss the wedding. We were sitting in the rockers on my front porch, drinking coffee and watching the waves crashing on the beach.

"Dixie, I want you to be my maid of honor."

"What? Are you serious?"

"Yes, I am. The past few months you have become the most important friend in my life. You were the one person that actually encouraged me in my relationship with Bob. Even my own mother told me to move on." She looks sad for a moment and then in typical Michelle style, she lights up again. "I mean, it had been eight years." We both chuckle a little.

"Let me guess, they said you were spending your best years with someone who obviously didn't love you the way you deserved."

"That and that I was wasting the baby-making years."

"Michelle, I would be honored to be your maid of honor. I love you and Bob, and you just need to remember that your best years haven't gotten here yet. Your best years will be every year the two of you are together because you are two halves of the same person."

Her eyes are full of tears as she reaches over and squeezes my hand. I am so full of joy for this beautiful, loving woman that I feel like my heart will burst. In my mind's eye, I picture chubby-cheeked little blond toddlers that will call me Aunt Dixie, and it brings me so much comfort.

She wipes her eyes with her napkin and then drops the next bomb on me. "One other thing, sweetie, can you also sing our wedding song?"

After sputtering and coughing on my tea, we got down to planning, and it was more fun than I would have thought possible.

Forty Two

It's the Saturday of Mardi Gras weekend, and I am having an honest to goodness girls' weekend. Cindy, Marsha, Michelle, and I are sitting on my balcony, overlooking the partying mass of people below. We have big baskets of beads sitting between our chairs, and we're having a blast tossing them down to the crowds. I have tied back the flowers and ferns so we would have a better view. The air is perfect, just a slight crispness that makes the crazy hats we are wearing very comfortable additions.

"Oh my, Dixie, do you know that man down there staring up at us?" Michelle asks, and I see immediately that it is Kevin. He is standing across the street on the sidewalk and is, indeed, looking straight up at the balcony. I am so used to him being in costume that I am momentarily taken off guard by how sexy he looks in his tight jeans and V-neck sweater.

"Kevin!" I yell and he grins and walks directly below the balcony.

"Dixie, Dixie, let down your hair!" He and I both laugh at this. "Can I come up? It seems you are surrounded by the most beautiful Mardi Gras fairies the city has ever seen!"

I grin at his theatrical flair. "If you promise to keep your fangs put away, then by all means, come on up!"

Instead of coming to the door, however, he begins climbing the wrought-iron lattice poles as he does when showing off for the tour crowds. The girls squeal in excitement over this show of raw manliness. I can feel the atmosphere change. Girls always get a little edgy when a good-looking, virile male is present.

"Kevin, these are my best girlfriends—Cindy, Marsha, and Michelle. Girls, this is my dear friend Kevin. He is the best ghost-tour leader in New Orleans."

He gives a dramatic bow and says "I would argue, but she speaks the truth." He then kisses the hand of each girl, and he lingers just a little longer with Marsha.

Hmmm. That could be interesting. Marsha is single and has never shown any interest in dating since I've known her. She is short and has a lean, muscular frame, most of which is covered with tattoos. She looks like she could kick anybody's butt. She has a very classical-style face and a short pixie haircut. She looks like Audrey Hepburn if Audrey Hepburn had been a biker chick.

I study her face when Kevin kisses her hand, and I spot the tell-tale spots of color in her cheeks that signal attraction.

"Kevin, can I get you a beer or whiskey maybe? I've got some Lazy Magnolia Southern Pecan, which is what we're drinking." I offer.

"Sure, Dix, that sounds great." I open the patio doors and leave them open to make the entertaining space bigger. Michelle has stepped in to help me arrange some chairs. On my way back out of the kitchen with more beers to put into the ice tub, I notice the television is still on even though the Bose is playing a blues playlist. I go over to turn it off just as a familiar face comes on the screen. I hear Michelle suck in her breath behind me, and I reach over to turn the volume up.

There is a pretty little reporter interviewing people on their way in to a charity Mardi Gras ball in Los Angeles. Everyone is in their finery, including the reporter as she gets talking points for *Access Hollywood*.

"Mason! Mason McCoy, over here." She beckons him over, and as he approaches, she asks him about the movie. "Mason, we know that filming is under way on your movie *African Sky*, and we want to know how it's coming along."

"Well, Mindy, first let me say that it is a dream come true to be filming this movie," he says this with his signature lop-sided grin. I can see through the screen the blush starting at the reporter's mostly exposed chest and moving up her neck. "And getting into character has been an adventure of a lifetime."

"Tell the viewers what has been the best tool for getting into the mind of Special Agent Aloysius Guerin?"

"Well, reading the books about ten times each put me a step ahead of the competition. But for getting into his mind, well, I have a very special friend to thank for that. She made me a playlist of music that she felt would be on Aloysius's iPod. I believe one of the best ways to get into another person's personality is through their taste in music."

I feel my breath catch in my throat. So now I know that he got the gift I left for him.

"A very special woman in your life, Mason? Who is she? Are you in love?" I can practically feel the excitement pouring through Mindy at the thought of a scoop. He walks off, then stops, and turns around.

"You know I'm not going to tell you who, Mindy. But I will tell you that she is very special although it was very recently that I realized *just* how special. And as for being in love, well, I don't deserve the right to be in love with her." Then he walks off.

I flip the set off and stare at the blank screen for several seconds. Then I turn to look at Michelle and see that Cindy is standing there as well.

"What the heck kind of answer was that?" Michelle demands. I feel her pain there. My insides are knotted, and yet, at the same time, I feel that familiar feeling of warmth spreading through my chest.

Forty Three

Late that night, I'm lying in my bed listening to the muffled sounds of the die-hard revelers on the street below. Cindy left an hour ago. She had just enough beers that she got sappy and wanted to see Dale. I thought that was sweet. Marsha and Kevin left together to go get breakfast, or maybe that would be a really late dinner. Michelle is sleeping soundly on my pullout sofa; all in all it was a successful, fun girl's night.

But now I can't sleep because I am thinking about what Mason said. It seems as though he may have reached a breaking point and could be softening in his willingness to accept forgiveness. I pray that should that be the case, that forgiveness for himself is part of it.

I give up on sleep and sit up against the headboard. I grab my iPad and fire up a playlist of some classical cello suites to soothe my nerves, which have been jumpy since seeing Mason's face on my television earlier. Pulling up my e-mail server, I see that I have thirty-eight new e-mails and start going through them, eliminating the sale ads, and then, there it is—an e-mail from the job.net address.

Dixie,

Sorry is a tired, worn-out word, definitely not sufficient for the remorse I have over the things I said at that dinner party. I have no excuse, other than I am a hideously flawed human.

Regardless of what I said, I cherish the e-mails you sent. I have read them many times. In fact I carry hard copies with me; and even though it took me a long time, I believe I finally understand how you can be forgiving toward me.

I read the verses you suggested in your e-mails. Dixie, I was raised in church, but I never really understood how the whole Jesus thing worked—the sacrifice and the forgiveness and the fulfillment of the law. When you pointed out in one of the notes about how even the prostitute, the killer, and the thief were all forgiven, it started to sink in that I couldn't out-sin His forgiveness. Even more, He forgave the very people who beat and killed Him. See, I believe the problem before was that I had heard the stories and read the chapters, but I had not seen the proof with my own eyes. Until you. You walked into my life and are the embodiment of that forgiveness Jesus had for us. Without cause I hated you, maligned your character, and then stood back while the most horrible, awful tragedy came raining down on you. But you forgave me without asking for anything in return. I'm still trying to wrap my head around that.

So now I understand how you can be forgiving. I really do, but I am still not quite comfortable with myself. I don't think I can be good for you, not right now, and I am not willing to take the chance of becoming enemies, and as I showed you and your friends on Christmas Eve, I don't do a great job of expressing my feelings.

All I have to offer right now is my apologies and my friendship.

Mason

I reread the e-mail three times. I have cried as much as I can over the last few months, so I am dry-eyed, but I am touched somewhere deep inside. I hit reply, and it is a simple message.

Mason,
  It's enough. I accept.

Dixie

Forty Four

On the way back to Bay St. Louis Sunday afternoon, Michelle and I are uncharacteristically quiet. We are both tired and thinking about our own separate issues. Just as I am exiting I-10, I slam on my brakes as a small black animal darts out in front of me.

"Holy cow!" Michelle screams.

"What was that?" I ask, not really expecting her to know.

"It looked like a dog," she answered and then she points out her window, "There it is." I follow her finger to a cowering little black shape in the ditch next to the road.

Against my better instincts, I jump out of the car and make my way over to the animal. He looks up at me, and I can see that he is shaking, and his tail is tucked. He is easily twenty-five pounds, but has a distinct puppy look to him.

I kneel on my haunches and make *tsking* sounds while holding my hand out. He initially backs away, but I don't move away, and I don't stop. Within a couple minutes, he has inched his way to me and is sniffing my hand. Still, I wait until he is licking my fingers, and then I take a chance and start scratching his head, and soon he is sitting in my lap, and I am getting my entire face licked.

"He is adorable!" I didn't even hear Michelle approaching. I've lost my heart to this little guy.

I smile up at Michelle. "He is, isn't he?" Then I get up awkwardly while holding the little guy in my arms. "Do you think it would be okay to take him with us?"

Michelle looks at the big paws and ears with a skeptical eye. "Do you know how big he's going to get?"

"I don't care. I mean, look at these eyes!" I see her melt as she looks into his sweet puppy face, and I can tell she has fallen, as well.

"Well, Dixie, you need to take him by the vet and make sure he's not micro-chipped and get him checked out"—she looks between me and the dog—"but I think this cutie may be just what you need."

"I think you're right."

When we get home, I take the puppy into the cottage and put a small bowl of water on the floor on top of a towel. He goes after it with so much gusto that I can't help but laugh at him.

In the fridge, I pull out some leftover chicken and cut it up with a sweet potato. This I put in a bigger bowl and sit on the floor next to me. He comes over, and he starts eating so fast I worry that he's going to choke.

"Hey there, little guy, slow down!" He looks up at the sound of my voice and jumps up and swipes my chin with his tongue. "I know, I know. I kind of like you too." He goes back to eating, and I watch him while contemplating a name. He's mostly black with white tips on his ears, tail, and toes. His eyes are light brown and soulful, and one of his ears sticks straight up while the other flops over, giving him a quizzical look.

"What shall I name you, little man?" He barely glances up at me as he licks the bowl clean then lies down on floor next to me and promptly falls asleep.

I start going through names, saying them out loud to see how they feel.

"Fido. Rover. Scout." No, a normal dog name won't work. "Norman. Dexter. Sammy. Elvis." I look down at him to see if he has an opinion, but his eyes are still closed. "You need a good strong name, baby boy. How about Duke or Maverick. Bogart. Bronson." Suddenly his head pops up and gives a short bark.

"Bronson? You like that name?" He turns his head to one side and grins at me. "Well, then, Bronson it is."

Later that night as I try to get to sleep with a warm body curled against the backs of my legs and the soft snuffling sounds of a dog in deep sleep, I pray to God and thank Him for my many blessings and especially for this unexpected gift and the joy it has brought me.

Forty Five

On the way into school the next morning, I drop Bronson off with a local vet, Dr. Kincy. He is a sweet man who obviously loves his job and agrees to check Bronson out even though we don't have an appointment.

"I'll give him a good once-over to figure out his age and then get his shots up-to-date."

"Can you tell me what breed he is, Dr. Kincy?"

"Well, best I can tell, I would say he's at least half black Lab judging by the webbed feet. The other half is harder to tell, but I think it could be border collie."

"How big do you think he'll get?"

"Oh, I'd say about eighty to one hundred pounds, judging by the size of his feet."

I can't do anything but gulp as he chuckles at me.

Later that day at school, Sandy comes by my office in the choir room. Things have been a little odd between us since the story about my identity came out. I know it put her, Johnny, and the kids in an awkward situation.

"Hey, Sandy, what's up?"

"Well, I was hoping you could tell me. Johnny got a call from Mason last night. He's coming for a visit, says he wants to spend some time with Colton and plan a trip to New York to visit the Julliard campus."

I close the folder containing the spring gala program. I am very pleased. Mason reconnecting with his family is a great step for him. "That's great news. I'm sure Colton will be excited for that to happen."

"He is. He adores his uncle Mason and puts a lot of weight on Mason's opinions." She takes her glasses off and rubs the bridge of her nose.

"Look, I don't completely understand what all has happened between the two of you the last few months. I don't need to know either." She smiles at me at reaches over and puts her hand on mine before continuing, "But I am thankful to you for not giving up and for not running away."

"Like I did last time?"

"It was your right to run away, dear. You had a right to this time, as well."

"Last time I had to heal myself in every sense of the word."

"And this time you're out to heal Mason?"

"No, I can't heal Mason, Sandy." I say with raised eyebrows. "I just want to help him heal himself."

She nods her head as she grasps my meaning. "Thank you," she says as she rises from her seat. I walk her to the doorway and watch her as she turns the corner back toward the office, then I close the door and slide down to the floor.

"Lord, I don't know what I have done to deserve the blessings you keep handing out, but thank you." I lower my head into my arms and picture Mason's face; not the angry, sardonic face from Paul and Randy's dining room but the face from the first time he visited the cottage—open and kind.

Forty Six

That night, I hook my new leash on Bronson's new collar, and we set out for a run along the beach. He is good for a bit but then gets distracted by the sea gulls, so we turn and head back. I am enchanted by the pure puppiness of the little guy; he is enthusiastic about every little sight and sound and creature we come across.

Once home, I grab a beer from the bridge, and get the tennis ball I purchased at the vet's office along with some very expensive but wholesome dog food. Bronson has thus far cost as much as a decent guitar, but I would gladly have spent twice as much.

Sitting on the porch, I start throwing the ball short distances, and sure enough, the lab in him takes over, and he retrieves it every time. The only obstacle we have to overcome is getting him to give it back to me, but Dr. Kincy gave me a book on Labs and tells me that, as a breed, they are very eager to please, and he should be easy to train. Thinking back on the two puddles and at least three piles I have had to pick up, I certainly hope this is true.

While I am practicing the art of playing fetch, my phone rings. I am expecting it to be Michelle, but to my surprise, it is Kevin's number on my caller ID.

"Hey, Kevin," I say by way of greeting. "Please don't tell me that you've bitten Marsha, and she's growing fangs."

He laughs at me but not as hardily as I would normally expect from him. Uh-oh, this must be serious.

"No, no biting. But I do want to talk to you about her."

I bite my lip and pump my fist in the air then calmly ask, "Sure, Kev, what's up?"

"I really like her, Dix."

"Great! That's awesome, Kev. She's a great girl."

"Is she? Cause I can't get her to talk about herself much. She would make a great poker player because she gives nothing away."

I think about tough, tiny little Marsha and the wall of steel she has around her. She gives very little up and then only after she completely trusts you. It took several months of friendship and late night talks for her to open up. This, in retrospective, was more than I ever did.

"Like all of us, Marsha has a lot of pain and hurt in her past. Her childhood was crap, and she joined the military at a very young age. She definitely holds her emotions close to the vest, but I can tell you this, she is worth the time it will take you to get through her walls."

"Do you think she will let me in?"

"Do you have plans to see her again?"

"Yes, she invited me to the bar on my night off."

"Well, that's the first time I know of her bringing a man there. In fact, you are the first man I know of that she has been out with since I've known her."

I can hear the smile in his voice when he says, "Really huh."

"Yes, really, you sexy vampire, you." I chuckle. "Is this Kevin Hart I'm talking to? I'm starting to wonder what happened to the man I know who can make ladies fall in love while simultaneously getting their wits scared out of them."

"Ah, Dixie, you always know how to make me feel better, sugar."

"Someone has to look out for your best interests. But fair warning, you hurt this girl, you'll have hell to pay."

"Hmmm, Dixie Bryan on the warpath." He makes shuddering noises on the other end, and we both end up laughing at the image.

"Thanks, Dix."

"Any time, Kevin. Let me know how it goes Wednesday."

When I hang up, I wrap my arms around my knees and hug them tight. I feel a joy deep down in my soul for these two special people. It seems there is love all around me.

Forty Seven

The week contains many errands related to Michelle's wedding. We have dress fittings, cake tastings, and venue visits. I don't think that I knew exactly what was going to be involved with being the maid of honor; my wedding was controlled by the iron fist of David's mother. I just showed up.

Today, I am planning to stay after school to work on a song for the wedding. My plan is to create a mash up of "At Last" and "Come Fly with Me" and I am very excited about it. After the last class of the day, I do a little work on grading and putting a test together for the musical direction class.

By the time I head to the choir room, I can hear the sound of the piano. I wonder who might be in there, and when I walk in, I see that it is Colton. I don't quite recognize the song he is playing before he sees me and stops playing. He has a guilty look on his face like I've caught him doing something wrong.

"Hey, Colton, I'm happy to see you!" I say this because it is true. Colton is one of my favorite students, and I love that he is putting extra time in. "Are you working on your Julliard submission?"

He gets the oddest expression on his face and then says, "Uh, yeah, Miss Bryan. I'm just going through a couple of ideas." He starts to get up, and I stop him.

"No, don't go anywhere. You can stay. I can do what I need to do at home."

"Are you sure? I could come in early tomorrow," he offers.

"Yes, of course." I smile at him because he is just so sweet. I decide to change the subject. "Are you excited about your trip with your Uncle Mason?"

He grins and says, "I sure am! Uncle Mason knows his way around New York City real well, and he says he'll show me all the cool spots and best restaurants."

"That's great, Colton. New York can be such an intimidating city, so to have that kind of guidance will be priceless."

"You've been there before?" he asks.

"I went to college in New England, and made a few treks to the city, yes." I think back to younger, more innocent times. "It's a wonderful place, and I can't wait to hear what you think about it."

He looks up at me in a way that reminds me so very much of his uncle and then asks, "Miss Bryan, do you love my Uncle Mason?"

Whoa, not the question I was expecting. "Well, yes, Colton, I do love your Uncle Mason. That's the simple answer, anyway."

He looks down at his hands resting on the keys and slowly nods his head. "My mom told me some of what happened between you guys. She said that Uncle Mason had a lot of baggage to work through before he could love you back." He looks up at me, and his eyes hold a lot of wisdom in them, showing me that he is much more observant than I have given him credit for. "I know what happened back then, and I know what happened to you, Miss Bryan. I don't know how you were able to forgive him, but I'm happy you did."

"Me too, Colton, and I was only able to do it because God helped me."

"'I can do all things through Christ who strengthens me', that's one of my favorite verses."

"I love that one too. I have leaned on it many times over the past couple of years." I look at him closely, and I can see that this is important to him. "Look, I need you to understand that people make mistakes, Colt. Sometimes there are major consequences, and sometimes it goes almost unnoticed. What your Uncle Mason did, well, let's just say he never thought it would go as far as it did. I understand that because I have been guilty of using hurtful words and not thinking through my actions at times in my life." I sit down next to him on the piano bench. "I guess what I'm trying to say here is that humans sin and goof up all the time, but falling in love is special and transcends our flaws."

He is listening intently now. I try my best not to mess this up. "Let me ask you a question. As humans, aren't we sinful, wretched beings?"

"Yes, ma'am."

"Does God love us regardless?"

"Of course."

"Okay, but why is it that he can love us regardless of the wrong that we do?"

"Because Jesus came and fulfilled the law so we could be forgiven."

"Exactly. Forgiveness is what made the way for us to experience His love."

I see the minute that he understands what I'm saying. He grins at me then. "So what you are saying is that the love you have for Uncle Mason wasn't dependant upon your forgiveness of him. It just allowed you to get to the forgiveness."

"Yes. You will discover soon enough that love rarely makes sense, and there is no use fighting it. Life will be much easier if you just go with it."

I put my arm around his shoulder and squeeze a little. He grins at me, and then I ask him to tell me his thoughts of my wedding-song choices.

Forty Eight

The month of March is like a runaway train heading straight for the spring gala and the wedding. The leisurely days of my first few months in Bay St. Louis are just a memory, and now I struggle to find the time to fit work, practice, wedding details, and walking Bronson into my days. I love it though. I would take cramming all this into a twenty-four hour day versus the lonely solitude of my self-imposed exile any day.

It's the Tuesday before Thursday-night's gala performance, and I am running with Bronson before getting ready for school. The sun is just peeking over the Bay Bridge as we run down the beach. In the short time I've been working with him, Bronson has become a terrific running partner. He no longer pulls on his leash, and he understands that there is a time for running and a time for chasing the birds. At the end of each run, I let him off the leash, and he spends a good fifteen minutes causing havoc amongst the flocks. He never even gets close, but it doesn't dampen his enthusiasm one bit.

Back home, I dispose of the doggie bag in the outside bin, and Bronson sets to work on his breakfast while I pour my giant mug of coffee. I'm going to need it is as today is the final run-through of the show, and I expect it to be a long day. Any fixes have to happen today as I have told the students that tomorrow is for resting their voices and relaxing. I don't want the nerves or the overthinking that comes from too many rehearsals.

At six that evening, I finally pack up my bag and head for the parking lot. I was excited about the gala all along, but now I am seriously stoked. The kids have worked so hard and are really ready to show the town what they are capable of. We are going to blow their socks off with some of the numbers we have planned. I find myself grinning like a fool as I drive home, and it lasts all the way through Bronson's walk.

At bedtime, Bronson and I curl up in my big bed. While I grab the iPad and start scrolling through e-mails, Bronson lays his head on my thigh and watches my every movement until the sandman gets the better of him.

The eighth e-mail in the list is from Mason. Even after all this time, my heart thumps uncomfortably in my chest, and I sit and stare at it for a while. The subject line says, simply, "Hello." I tamp down a feeling of mild irritation because I don't need this distraction right now. I am at a point where my emotions are wrung out. But my resolve not to open the e-mail lasts for less than five minutes.

> Dearest Dixie,
> Thank you for your return e-mail. I will probably never be able to express how much it meant to me.

I also want to tell you how much your mentoring of Colton has meant to me personally. I love that kid and am very excited that he may be able to do what he loves as a career. I had Bob pushing me and then I had a Drama teacher, Mr. Staten, who encouraged me to pursue my passion. Without them I wouldn't be where I am today; I feel like you are that person for Colt.

I told you once that I thought you were going to be an amazing teacher. As I have a bad habit of doing, I underestimated you.

I am looking forward to the Gala; I hope I can see you while I'm there.

Your friend,
Mason

I reread the e-mail three times. I'm trying to gauge my feelings and am incredibly surprised by the butterflies in my stomach. My infatuation seems to be as strong today as it was the night of our first kiss. It's so frustrating and at the risk of sounding like a girl. I don't understand how he can not be as affected as I am. In fact, the more I think about it, the madder I get. I type out several responses, but each time I'm about to hit send, I talk myself out of it and promise myself that after I've slept on it, I will figure out something to say back.

But I don't, and Wednesday passes by in a blur and still I don't answer. I just don't think I can face it right now. Maybe I will see him tomorrow, and maybe I won't, but until the gala is over, I can't focus enough to address him.

Forty Nine

Half an hour before show time on Thursday, and I am running around tying on bows and straightening ties. The kids are much calmer that I am. Ironic since I will be standing in the wings while they do all the work.

Five minutes until the curtain goes up, I peek out at the audience. Nearly every seat is taken, and I am thrilled for the kids. I want them to feel like their hard work is paying off and doesn't go unnoticed. Just as I am about to turn and go backstage again, I see a familiar figure enter the back doors and make his way down the center aisle toward his brother- and sister-in-law. My heart jumps even farther up into my throat, and my mouth goes dry. I'm going to have to get over this before the final act. I'm singing "It's a Man's World" with several of the students as the finale.

The first act is Colton. He's playing and singing Billy Joel's "Piano Man," which will run straight into all the boys singing "Ain't No Sunshine." Then both the boys and girls will sing a mash-up of "Somebody to Love" and "Why Can't this Be Love" then go into a funny mix of "Paradise by the Dashboard Light" and "It Ain't Me, Babe." The kids have had a blast putting the numbers together, and it shows by how fabulously they deliver.

As I take the stage for the final number, dressed in the costume of a man's trousers, shirt, suspenders, and completed by a fedora hat, I am relaxed and confident because of how well the night has gone. The girls are confident, and they rise to the occasion and very nearly make me unnecessary to the number, but I enjoy it all the same. At the last verse, all the boys join us on stage, and we reach the grand finale and receive a standing ovation. The kids are over the moon with the reaction, and I am so proud of them I can't help but get a little teary-eyed.

Afterward, I stay backstage until the last of the kids have changed and all the costumes are put away. I am planning to head over to Michelle's house for drinks with her and Bob. They were here at the performance, and Michelle has been a great supporter through all the preparations. More than one night over the past few months, she would bring me dinner at the school while I worked late on the music.

In the parking lot, there are still a few people talking around their cars, and the sound of laughter hangs in the air. As I pass a pick-up truck and see my car, I immediately notice the figure leaning up against it. It's a silhouette that I would know anywhere and my heart starts beating more rapidly.

"Hi," he says as I approach. He seems a little unsure of himself.

"Hello," I reply.

"That was a heck of a show you and the kids put on."

"Thank you. I have been so blessed with these talented kids. They are a pure pleasure to work with."

"I think they have an awesome teacher too."

I can't help it. I blush under his praise and then to make matters worse, I get angry turning my face even redder. How can I still be so affected by him?

"Well, thank you, Mason."

"Colton awed me tonight, Dixie. I can't even comprehend how he is this talented, and we didn't realize it."

"He just needed a little encouragement to really let loose and understand that he didn't need to fit anyone else's mold."

"That's what makes you such a great teacher, Dixie, you always encourage others to be exactly who they are supposed to be, not what they think they should be."

I let out a huge sigh and look down at the ground. "Everybody but me, huh?"

"That's not what I meant. I get why you didn't tell the truth about your identity."

"Mason." I run my hands through my hair as I try to think of the best way to address this. "I don't know if you can believe this, but other than my name, I was more honest with my emotions and feelings with you than I have been with anyone ever."

He cocks his head and narrows his eyes.

"My parents were both challenged when it came to emotions. They had a social disorder that kept them from having the correct responses to situations. So it took me years of living with my grandparents to learn how to interact with my peers, but until you, I had never talked about my feelings in any real depth." I look back at him now before I add, "Not even my husband."

"If you're trying to take some blame for that explosion, Dixie, then just stop it. Even when I was saying those stupid things, I didn't really believe them."

"Regardless, I need you to understand that I meant every word I said to you, and my reactions were completely honest."

"Speaking of honest, I have wanted to ask you a few things on the subject of the Bible."

I am surprised but pleased by this turn of subject. "All right."

He hesitates, stops, and then starts again, "As a scientist, how do you explain creation? Don't you believe in evolution? And if you do, does that mean the rest of the books are allegorical?"

I think about this for a few seconds. There is so much that I could say here, but I need to pack as much into as little as possible. "As a scientist, as you say, I had an intimate look into the sheer genius of our Creator, Mason." I grin at him before I go on. "Our bodies are made so wonderfully complex that there is no way it was happenstance. Let me ask you a question. Do you know how many amino acids it takes to make one strand of protein?"

He raises his eyebrows and says, "I must have missed that class in school."

I laugh at him. "It's okay, only us science geeks took those classes. The answer is at least sixteen for the most basic of living organisms, and they have to be exactly the right ones to work together. Then, proteins make up all the other cells, including DNA. And there are around 450 *trillion* strands of DNA in the human body. Now, before your eyes glaze over, my point here is that in order to believe the Theory of Evolution or the Big Bang Theory, you have to believe that exactly the right sixteen amino acids managed to get together to create a viable protein, and then that happened again and again until you had enough to create DNA strands. Mason, the chances of those amino acids binding together to create the very first protein are ten to the power of forty. In other words, you could reduce all the world's rainforest to the amino acid level and still not get the necessary combination of acids."

I look at him and see that he is surprised by this information.

"That is just one of hundreds of scientific facts that led me to believe in intelligent design. There's also the fact that every single tribe and race of people known have historical stories about a world-wide flood and a patriarchal figure that survived in a giant boat. But, Mason, you can't believe just because of what I say. You need to pray and study and find your own answers. Trusting in God is a personal journey, and if you truly want the answers, He will lead you to them."

"Okay, fair enough. One more question if I may?"

I hold my hands open to indicate he should go for it.

"I know that Randy and Paul are two of your close friends, but what do you think God's feelings about gay people are?"

Eeeek. Creation and homosexuality in one conversation. Maybe his middle name is Ram.

"Keep in mind that the Bible is in two distinct sections—before Christ and after. Before, all sin had an earthly judgments and the repentance and punishment was very harsh. For whatever reason, many Christians today hang on to certain sins as being *worse* than others, which is ridiculous. Christ came to fulfill the law and bring forgiveness for all sins. If we accept Him, God looks at us through the blood of Christ and sees no sins, regardless of whether it's lies, murder, or sexual sins."

"So you believe gay people can be Christians?" His eyebrows are raised as if he is in disbelief.

"I know they can, Mace. If they believe in Him and love Him and truly want His forgiveness, of course they will be forgiven."

"Are Randy and Paul Christians?"

"You know, Mace, it's ultimately between them and God, but they say they love Jesus, and they attend services. They don't live a wild, salacious lifestyle. You know, Mace, Jesus says in chapter 7 of Matthew that you will know His children by their fruit. If you were to spend time with either of those men without knowing they were a couple, what would you think of them?"

"That they are two of the most giving, loving, and charitable men I've ever met."

"Exactly. Sin is in our DNA Mason. We can't escape it. We can only go to the One who paid our debt and then try our best to follow His example. The sheer simplicity is what throws most folks off."

"So you're saying there is no one that can't be a Christian?"

"That's right. Anyone who acknowledges Him as their Savior and asks for it will be forgiven." My heart is leaping for joy over these questions because they show that he is being led to investigate.

"Tell you what, I will e-mail you some links and names of books I think will help you with your questions."

He takes a couple steps forward and pulls me into an embrace. Slowly, I relax against him. I feel so warm and safe in his arms.

All too soon, he releases me. "I have to go. Johnny and Sandy are having a party for Colton."

"I understand. I'm headed to Michelle and Bob's for drinks."

We smile at each other, and his eyes search mine. I don't look away, and I try to make my face as open as possible, but I don't say anything further. Instead, I reach up and cup his jaw and smooth a lock of his ebony hair back from his forehead. My own jaws ache from wanting to kiss his lips but settle for his cheek before walking off and getting into my car and driving away. Two blocks pass before my eyes fill with tears, and I say a quick prayer of thanks for restoring some of the friendship we had built, and for giving him a curiosity to learn more about the Savior. If nothing ever develops beyond that, I would be able to accept it.

Fifty

The last day of school dawns bright and warm. It's Wednesday in the second week of May, and the kids are more than ready to be free to roam the beaches and earn money at summer jobs.

My classes are bittersweet as we recall our past performances and the friendships we have made. My Glee Club kids sing summertime songs, and we plan to get together a couple times over the summer break to work on programs for the autumn festival.

I know I will see a few of them in a couple days at Michelle and Bob's wedding, and I draw comfort from that. In a town as small as BSL, it will be inevitable that I will see them at their summer jobs and the various festivals in town.

I am hosting a bachelorette party for Michelle this Thursday night at my house, and I'm really looking forward to it. We don't have plans to get wild, but it will still be nice to have all day Friday to relax and get ready for the Saturday-afternoon wedding. The weather is supposed to be beautiful, which is great news for the outdoor reception we have planned to take place behind the church after the wedding. There will be a large dance floor with columns at each corner, with yards and yards of tulle and flowers crisscrossed between them. The area is surrounded by large magnolia and live oak trees from which will be hung dozens and dozens of paper lanterns. The flowers that we have chosen are of the most fragrant varieties to make it as pleasing as possible for Bob.

I have called upon Dale and his students to come cater the event, and the menu is stunning—barbeque shrimp, red beans and rice, crawfish ettoufee, and gumbo among other items. They are also bringing a wedding cake that resembles a work of art that incorporates Michelle's colors of bronze and silvery blue. Bob's groom cake is red velvet with cream cheese icing and promises to be a culinary delight.

I have thoroughly enjoyed planning this big day with Michelle, and like any production, I am very much looking forward to it all coming together.

Fifty One

Thursday night, I welcome Michelle and some of her real-estate friends into my house, along with Cindy and Marsha who have become good friends to Michelle since our adventure on Mardi Gras weekend. We have lingerie gifts and make fun frozen drinks and the conversations get a little bawdy as everyone starts giving Michelle grief about the honeymoon. Michelle starts trying to turn the tables, and her first diversion is Marsha's relationship with Kevin.

"Okay, okay, guys. I want to hear about Marsha's love life for a minute. How is it going with that hunk that climbed our balcony?"

Marsha's face gets a little pink, but she smiles broadly. "What can I say? He's perfect. At least for me he is." She looks over at me and then says, "I can't believe I'm in love with a man that plays dress up for a living! And one that play acts like a vampire, at that. It's almost a cliché."

"I am so happy for you, Marsha. Kevin is a fabulous guy!" I enthuse to her. "And so gorgeous too."

At that statement, all the women hoot and holler and demand to see photos. This is what happens at a girl-only party after all.

When everyone settles down, Michelle looks over at me and asks about the status of my relationship with Mason. I had told her and Bob about my run-in with Mason at the spring gala, and they were both so happy to hear that there had been progress made.

"Well, we've talked a few times since then but no plans have been made for us to see each other again." This is the truth, and it doesn't really bother me. We have picked up our old habits of talking on the phone for hours, sometimes about music. Other times just sharing stories from our past with each other. We have started a new topic for debate—best restaurants in cities we have both visited. That started after he took Colton to New York City, and I asked him where he had taken the boy to eat.

"Well, Dixie," Michelle says. "Mason is coming to the wedding, so you should see him Saturday."

I'm not shocked by this. Mason had told me that the filming on *African Sky* was set to be finished this week. Bob is one of Mason's oldest friends, so I would have been somewhat shocked had he not come. However, I had not talked to him about it because I was doing my best to not have any expectations. I had turned the situation over to God and trusted Him to work it out to fulfill His will.

"That's great, Michelle. I know how much that will mean to both of them."

"But what about you? How much will it mean to you?" She is insistent that I talk about this, and I can see that Cindy is very interested in my response as well.

"It will mean a whole lot actually. Don't get me wrong. I am very happy right now, and I will be happy no matter what happens. I've seen sorrow in its blackest cloak and nothing can make me unhappy after getting past that." I shudder slightly at the memory. "But I love Mason and am at my most settled when I'm with him, so of course, I will enjoy seeing him."

Cindy reaches over and lays her hand on mine. I know she is thinking of Dale and sympathizes with my feelings.

"Okay, enough of this talk, girls! We have games to play and then I have a variety of movie clips of the most romantic moments to ever happen on the big screen!" I announce and everyone starts talking and laughing.

The rest of the night goes by without any further mention of Mason McCoy, but his sultry blue eyes still manage to haunt my dreams when I finally fall asleep in my porch bed that night.

Fifty Two

S aturday morning dawns sunny and mild. The wedding is scheduled for 5 p.m., but I am expecting Michelle and the other bridesmaids around noon. We are having a light lunch and then getting our makeup and hair done by Jean-Luc and his partner, Mark. Michelle has stored her wedding dress in one of my spare bedrooms, and the bridesmaids are bringing theirs along. A photographer is going to be with us, taking pictures for the whole process. Michelle is planning to have tons of photos because even though Bob won't be able to see them, she can describe the memories, and their future children will be able to see the start of their parents' lives together.

Just as I am finishing some yoga on the platform in the backyard, I hear the doorbell. It's Michelle, and she is more than an hour early.

"Hi! I know I'm early, but I've been awake for hours, and I couldn't stay in that house for another minute!"

"Oh, sweetie, come on in here! I'm glad you came. The last thing we need is you overthinking the day." I usher her in to the kitchen where I pour her a glass of citrus water.

"Well, between my mom and my sisters, my nerves are frayed," she confesses. This is what I was afraid of for her.

"Well, welcome to the sea of tranquility, sweetie. From here on out, no more decisions, no more pressure. I promised Bob I would get you to the altar, on time and happy."

She grins at me and puts her hand over mine. "Thank God for you, Dixie. No way could I have done this without you."

"You could have, but there may have been bloodshed!"

We both laugh at this and then she sobers and there are tears in her eyes.

"I'm serious, Dixie. I have come to depend on you so much, and it's not really even fair. I'm never going to understand how you aren't just a big ball of bitterness, yet here you are—every bit as happy for me as I am."

I stare at her for a few beats, and then I smile as gently as I can. "I was for a long time, Michelle. There was a time that I would have been envious of you and the fact that you get to be married to a man you love and have his babies." No matter how much I don't want to I start to tear up. "But while I obviously still mourn those losses, I don't begrudge anyone else their happiness. I've learned to find happiness in the smallest aspects of my life and to be genuinely happy in others' good fortune."

"You're so wise, and I'm so glad we are friends." She looks at me in that way she has when she knows she's approaching a tough subject. "You would make such a great mom. Do you think you would ever adopt?"

"I really hope to. Someday maybe."

"Will you be the Godmother to mine?"

"Oh, Michelle, that's the sweetest thing anyone has ever asked me." Now the tears are streaming down my face. "I will love your children as if they were my own and do anything for them in my power." We embrace tightly, and then she abruptly releases me.

"Okay, enough of that. I'm starving! Whatcha got in the fridge?"

Fifty Three

A few hours later, I am standing behind Michelle as she takes in her own image in the large mirror in the guest bedroom. She is breathtakingly gorgeous in her simple white wedding dress. Her hair is trailing down her back and held up on the sides with beautiful jeweled combs that belonged to Bob's grandmother. Around her neck is a simple gold chain containing a floating heart, which was a gift from me for her bridal shower. Her ears have small but beautiful sapphire studs. They match her big round eyes perfectly. For her borrowed item, her mother brought the veil she wore in her own wedding, and it is the perfect final touch.

Right now, those big eyes are shimmering from unshed tears. "I wish that Bob could see me," she whispers. "Does that make me a horrible, selfish person?"

"Absolutely not, Michelle. I wish he could see you too." I smile at her over her shoulder. "But when you walk down the aisle, and he hears all the gasps when everyone gets a look at you, he'll know. He'll know that he is marrying a woman who is as beautiful on the outside as he knows you are on the inside." Now I am blinking rapidly to keep the tears from ruining the masterful job Mark did with my makeup. Luckily he gave us all waterproof mascara in anticipation. "Now, come on. Let's get in that limo and go get married!"

At the church, we sneak in a side door to meet Michelle's mom, dad, and sister. Her dad is visibly moved at seeing his baby girl in her wedding dress. This is going to be a very emotional day I can see. Just as I am starting to worry about my makeup again, the door opens and the pastor peeks in.

"Ya'll about ready? Everyone is seated, and Bob is waiting impatiently for his bride."

"Yes! Tell them to start the music. Mrs. Gibson, you and Brooke go take your seats." I herd them out the door then turn and look at Michelle, her dad, and the other two bridesmaids, Jill and Tracy.

"Remember, don't lock your knees, or you'll pass out." At the horrified looks on their faces, I can't help but bust out laughing as we enter the foyer.

When Michelle enters the chapel, I was right about the gasps. Every eye in the place was on her with the exception of two people; my eyes were glued to a set of blue eyes that had captured mine as soon as I turned around after reaching the altar. All the air left my lungs, and I was once again shocked at the response my body has to him. I feel almost relieved when I have to turn toward the pastor and break the connection.

After the ceremony, us girls go and get our makeup touched up for the photograph session. When we get back to the chapel, Bob and the groomsmen, which are his two brothers and one brother-in-law, are taking goofy pictures. It's a nice lighthearted moment, and we all join in, especially when it comes time for the marriage certificate pictures.

Just as we are about done, Bob pulls his cell phone out and makes a call and then asks the photographer to wait around for a few more minutes.

"I have an old friend I want a couple shots with."

Before the doors open, I know it's going to be Mason. When he strolls in, he goes straight to Bob and, like someone who's accustomed to being with the blind, he starts talking before he gets to Bob to let him know that he is approaching. They slap each others backs and speak softly to one another. When Mason turns, I can see the tears in his eyes at whatever it was that Bob had said.

A series of photos are taken with Mason, involving Bob and Michelle and the whole wedding party. Just as we are finished, Mason walks over to me.

"You look beautiful, Dixie. Bronze is definitely a good color on you."

"Thank you, Mason. We got lucky. Michelle has great taste in fashion."

He looks down at my feet and then back up at me. "Seeing you in those stiletto heels is doing something funny to my insides. Even if it is annoying how tall they make you." Then he gives me one of his lopsided smirks. I flush like a little girl, I can't help it.

"It's great you made it. Bob is obviously thrilled."

"What about you? Are you happy to see me?"

"I'm always happy to see you, Mason. I miss you, and the time we used to spend together."

"I do as well. You don't know how much I wish I could go back to the way things were before." He looks down at his hands as he says this.

"But they can't, Mason. It happened. We are who we are. You are capable of tearing down the wall between us, and when you do, I will be standing on the other side, ready to get on with what we started." I stare at the top of his bent head for a few seconds and then I take a step back.

"I need to run, Mace, I'm riding with the bridal party to the reception, and I'm singing the song for the first dance so I can't be late." I turn and walk few steps away and then my will deserts me, and I turn back around. "If you're going to be there, I would really like it if you would save a dance for me." His head snaps up, and he breaks out in a grin.

"I will look forward to it, Miss Bryan."

Fifty Four

When I stand up to sing for the first dance, I am wondering how I am going to get through it without crying. All the moments from the cake cutting to the speeches given by Michelle's father and Bob's brother have made my emotions high. Now, I'm singing the highly emotional song "At Last." Thank goodness I'm breaking it up with some lines from Sinatra's "Come Fly with Me."

In the end, the emotions made the performance better, and there wasn't a dry eye in the house by the time the couple had made just a few rotations around the dance floor.

As I walked off the raised stage, I saw Colton coming up the other side. When he sits down at the piano and starts playing, I realize that the day I walked in on him in the music room he must have been practicing for this performance; the notes are the same, but I didn't recognize the song then; now I do. He is playing the song "The Reason," and suddenly out of nowhere, Mason is in front of me holding his hand out.

"You ready for that dance? I believe he's playing our song."

I'm stunned, but I take his hand and walk on the dance floor. He pulls me close and puts one hand around my waist and holds mine with the other. Because of my heels, I am looking slightly down, but our gazes lock, and I am finding it hard to breathe right.

"I asked Colton to sing this song today, Dixie, because it says everything that I haven't been able to say." He smiles at me, and the butterflies take flight again. "I have come to terms with what happened, finally. Thanks to some counseling from Pastor White and time spent praying—really praying. Now I can't think of anything but you—your love, tolerance, and forgiveness. But also your eyes, smile, and your beautiful hair."

I smile through my tears at that. I realize the song is nearly over, and a bit of panic sets in because I know we will get caught up in the remaining festivities, and I want this to last forever.

"Mason, no matter what happens the rest of this night, will you do something for me?"

"Anything."

"Will you meet me at Tommy's Wine Bar in the Warehouse district tomorrow night?"

"What time?"

"Eight o'clock," I answer.

"Of course," he says, and then he reaches up and cups my face and gives me the sweetest kiss I've ever experienced.

Then, as I expected, we were separated by other dance partners and my maid of honor duties. We ran into one another during the garter toss, and got the chance to share another clandestine kiss while I was out in front of the church making sure the limo taking the couple to the airport was on time. Mason playfully pushed me inside the back of the limousine and climbed in behind me where for about five minutes, we acted like teenagers at a drive-in theatre.

Just before the bird seed toss, I am in the dressing room helping Michelle get her wedding dress off and traveling clothes on. She is glowing and happy, and I feel like I should split into two people just to contain my joy for her.

After we zip the dress into its hanging bag, she turns and hugs me spontaneously.

"I am so happy, Dixie!" she whispers in my ear.

"Me too, Michelle, me too."

"I saw Mason kiss you. Does that mean everything's worked out between you two?"

"I'm not really sure right now, but I do know that we have opened the door again."

"Well, promise me you won't go getting married while I'm in Boston."

"I'm confident that won't happen, darling."

I grab her toiletries bag, and we head out into the hallway where her family and Bob are waiting. While they discuss the run to the car, I go on out and stow the bag with the other suitcases and then stand back to watch the couple run the gauntlet.

Afterward, I am helping clean the reception area when there is a tap on my shoulder. When I turn, I find Sandy standing there, and she pulls me into an embrace.

"Dixie, I just wanted to thank you again for what you've done with Colton. He's so happy and fulfilled, and his dad and I are stunned at difference a few months have made."

I smile at her. "It's been my pleasure to work with him."

She searches my eyes before going on. "I also want to thank you for the patience you've shown with Mason and the way you've been able to get him to look at his relationship with God."

"That was just seed planting on my part. God watered and gathered."

"And so He did." She smiles and squeezes my hand. "Well, I couldn't leave without thanking you. I hope to see you some over the summer break.

With that, she was gone, taking the men of her family with her. I'm not sad, however, I have a date tomorrow night.

Fifty Five

The following evening at 7 p.m., I'm standing in front of the mirror in the bathroom of my New Orleans flat. I have the sides of my hair pulled up, and the back is a mass of curls. I have a small amount of makeup on but took extra time dressing. I decided on a yellow chevron print skirt that hits me just below the knees, a simple white tee and a pair of comfy white Keds tennis shoes. They are perfect for the stroll over to the warehouse district.

When I arrive at Tommy's, I sit at a corner settee and order a bottle of Honig Cabernet. The sound system is softly playing some Wes Montgomery, which is who Mason chose as his favorite jazz guitarist during one of our discussions. The thought of that conversation makes me smile to myself and just then the door opens and in he walks. While he gets his bearings and looks around, I have a few seconds to take him in.

His hair has gotten a bit long and hangs over the collar of his white dress shirt. It is dark and shiny like a raven's wing. He has a serious five o'clock shadow on his cheeks, which make his full pink lips all the more incongruent. His shoulders are broad, and his back is straight, and he carries himself like the confident man he is. His narrow hips are draped in beautiful parchment-colored linen pants that hang perfectly on him.

I gulp as I suddenly feel very plain and awkward in comparison. But the feeling lasts only a few seconds because as soon as his eyes find mine, they light up, and his features fill with joy.

He slides into the booth next to me, and without uttering a word, he takes my mouth prisoner in a soul-scorching kiss.

"I love when your mouth tastes like wine, my dear."

"Careful, sweetie, you're encouraging me to become a wino."

He throws his head back and laughs. "Oh, how I've missed you."

"You have me now, Mace, for as long as you want me."

His eyes narrow slightly and then widen. This action is what sends smoke signals to deep, hidden parts of my body.

"Do you mean that, Dixie? I mean, really mean it?"

Something in the sound of his voice causes me to lean in closer and study his face before I answer.

"Of course, I do. Against all odds and anything that makes sense in this world, I love you. You're who I think of before I go to sleep and the face I see in my dreams, Mason. Every fun and new thing I experience, the first thing I think is that I wish I could share it with you."

"I feel the same, Dix. Without you, food doesn't taste as good, wine isn't as exquisite, and the music is duller."

He grabs my hands in his, and suddenly, I feel like I'm underwater and can't breathe. "I've been meeting with Pastor White, and he's been counseling me through a few issues, and I've done lots of praying and believe I'm finally ready." He suddenly looks unsure and younger than his age.

"Dixie Bryan, I can hardly believe I'm doing this, but I don't think I will get a second of rest until I do." He reaches in his pocket and pulls out a small white box. Now I am seeing spots in my vision, but I still can't breathe.

"Will you marry me?" he says as he holds out the most beautiful square-cut diamond ring I have ever seen. I can't move. I can only stare and still I don't breathe.

"Dixie?" he asks, and the scared hope in his voice is finally what pulls me out of my stupor. I breathe in a great gulp of air and with it a shaking sob. I nod my head up and down, and his face breaks into a huge grin.

"Is that a yes? Please, Dixie, tell me yes."

"Yes, yes! Oh yes, Mason!" I launch myself at him then and am only vaguely aware that the patrons at the surrounding tables are clapping for us.

Suddenly, a thought comes to me, and I pull back. Instantly he freezes.

"Mason, when you said you had been praying and counseling with Pastor White, does that mean—"

"Yes, I am fully embracing Christ as my Savior. Every opportunity that I have, I will be sitting in the congregation, worshipping while my beautiful, talented wife sings her lungs out to the glory of God." With this, his face nearly breaks in two with his grin, and he leans over and kisses the tip of my nose.

Love feels good.

Fifty Six

Two days later, I'm lying in an enormous bed in Las Vegas next to a beautiful, but snoring man. I smile and lightly ruffle my hands through his hair without waking him. The last two days have been pure bliss, but I have a phone call to make to apologize to someone I broke a promise to.

On the third ring, she picks up. "Dixie, what's wrong? I know you wouldn't be calling me on my honeymoon unless something major is going on."

"I'm calling to beg your forgiveness, Michelle."

"What on earth for, sugar?"

"Well, you see, I'm on my honeymoon too!" Then I hold the phone away from my ear as she hoots through the line.

Several minutes later, I walk back into the bedroom of our penthouse suite to find Mason sitting up in the bed, watching me. I let the robe fall away before I crawl into the bed next to him. I'm still amazed by the love and hunger I see on his face when he looks at me.

"Michelle accept your apologies?"

"Yep," I say as I start running my hand through his chest hair. I have a sudden thought and look up at Mason. "Do you like dogs?"

He looks surprised for a second and then nods his head. "As a matter of fact, I do. I love all animals, actually."

"I don't know if I've told you that I got a dog. He's awesome. Huge but awesome. His name is Bronson."

"I can't wait to meet him. Are there any other surprises waiting for me?"

"Nope, but we probably need to talk about where we'll live at some point."

"Are you kidding me? I've been trying to figure out how to get access to that amazing swinging bed since the minute I laid eyes on it."

"I'm glad to hear that. Spending quality time together out there sounds like heaven on earth to me."

"Good. Now I have a question for you," he says in a throatier voice.

"What's that, dear husband?"

"What are we going to tell all the children we adopt about this giant tattoo on your back?"

"It's not giant!" I say indignantly, then the full impact of his words hit me, and my eyes fill with tears. He pulls me onto his chest and wipes the tears from my lashes.

"You are going to be an awesome mom, Dixie McCoy."

Lightning Source UK Ltd.
Milton Keynes UK
UKOW07f1453141214

243121UK00012B/146/P